Reuben, Reuben

Reuben, Reuben

a Hobo's Journals

Joanne Blakley

Library of Congress Control Number: 2021909585
ISBN: Hardcover 978-1-6641-7457-3
Softcover 978-1-6641-7456-6
eBook 978-1-6641-7455-9

This is a work of historic fiction. Characters, places, incidents, and dates are used creatively to tell a fictitious story and not to be taken as historic fact.

Print information available on the last page.

Rev. date: 05/18/2021

To order additional copies of this book, contact:
Xlibris
844-714-8691
www.Xlibris.com
Orders@Xlibris.com
830204

Contents

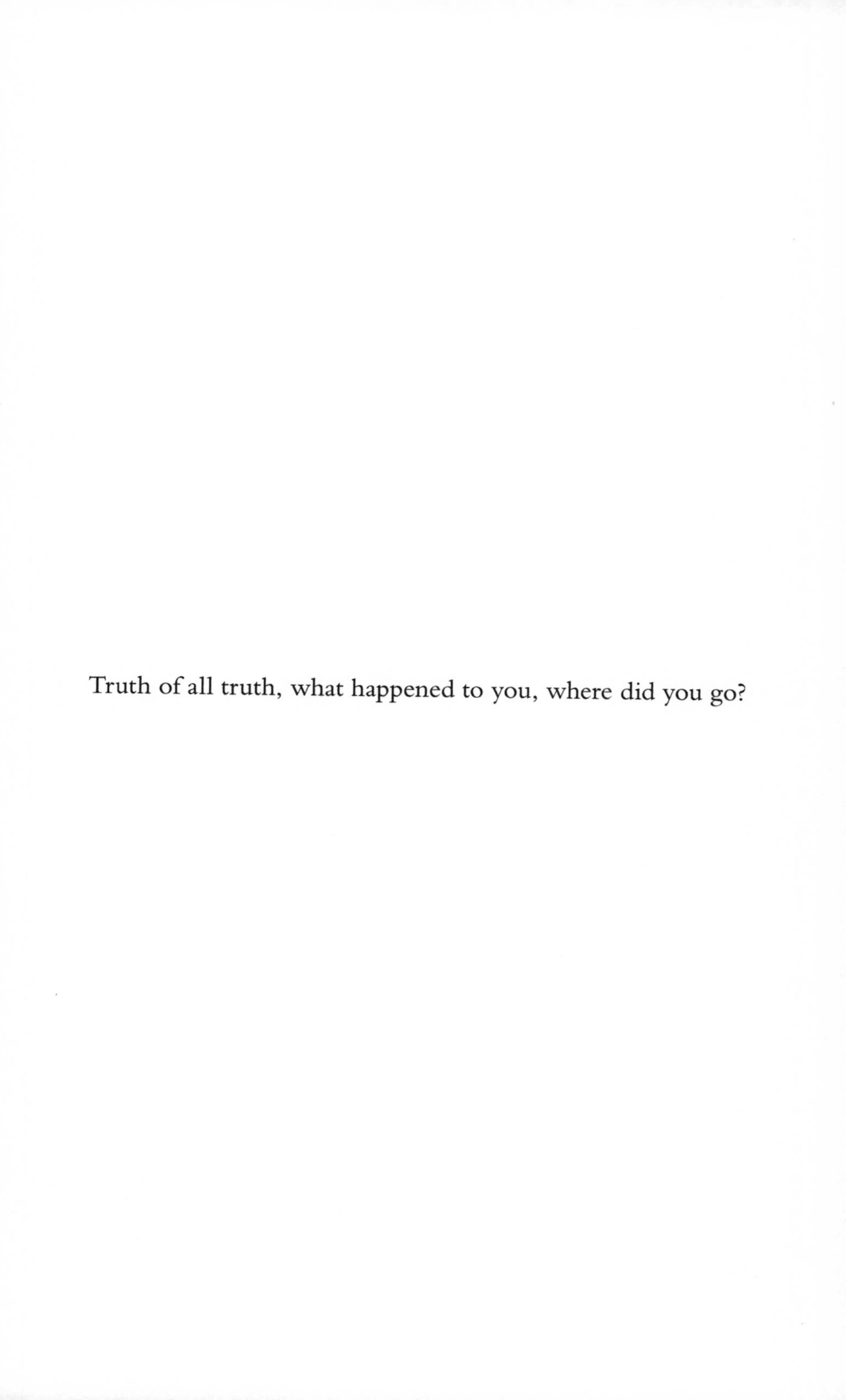

Truth of all truth, what happened to you, where did you go?

Preface

My grandfather Reuben Martinson escaped from a mental hospital in 1939 and was never seen or heard from again. After years of searching for clues, I decided perhaps the best way to have a sense of closure about his disappearance was to write a story of what *could* have happened. After researching that time period in America's history, I decided that it was quite possible that he became a hobo.

Reuben, Reuben, A Hobo's Journals, is a fictional accounting of a mentally-ill hobo poet, using real people and actual events as a framework to tell a story of the life of a traveling worker in the United States in the 1940's.

I attended the National Hobo Convention in Britt, Iowa, the second time camping in the jungle with my grandson. I was impressed by the quality of character I found, and the brotherhood that exists among hobos. I was especially pleased to learn that many hobos are poets and story tellers when they gather around the jungle fire. Reuben would have fit right in. I know I did.

Reuben's granddaughter,
Joanne Blakley

Acknowledgements

Heartfelt thanks to everyone who's helped along the way: Fran McBride, Hildur's daughter, John Perkins, the Farley teenager in 1940, Benny Noble who worked on an oil rig in Borger, Uncle Bob, Polly Ryan, and Caleb from George Ranch, Thelma Price, owner of Gladstone Mercantile, Leonard and Judy Flamm of Flamm's Orchards, and the librarians and historians in Anna, Cairo, Richmond, Pawhuska, Ponca City, Texhoma, Dixon, Pensacola, and Santa Fe.

A special thanks to my writing friends, Carol Dooley, Diane Skelton, Charlie Davis, Bonnie Cissell, Ann McMurphy, Christine Blakley, Sheila Hadaway, Lorren Steele, and members of West Florida Literary Association. I couldn't have done this without you.

And most especially, my mom Dorene Martinson, not just for sharing your memories but for giving me the sense of family unity that made this book necessary. This is for you.

Patient Records, Iowa Hospital for the Insane

Doctor's Notes (excerpts)

12/8/36 Reuben Martinson admitted from Vinton County Jail. Apprehensive, hands cold as ice. Keeps looking over shoulder; says someone is going to kill him. Starts as though hears voices. General appearance of subnormal mental type but fairly well informed and good at figures. Is quiet and tidy, oriented for time and place. Height 6'2", Weight 139 lbs.

3/27/37 Fair physical condition. Melancholic. Delusions of self-unworthiness. Diagnosis of Manic Depressive Psychosis.

7/1/38 Displays passive, compliant behavior. Does not make eye contact. Observed stereotypical behavior (rocking) in confinement room.

1/17/39 Suspected cheeking of pills.

5/21/39 Patient in excellent condition physically, well nourished. Good appetite. Weight 169 lbs. Adjusted, no sign of depression.

Ward Notes (excerpts)

12/8/36 New patient, looks scared to death, wrings hands, repeats "I've failed, I've failed." Very poor appetite.

2/21/37 Patient continues to be sad and withdrawn. Says he will never get better, says he's failed and ashamed and wants to die. Frequent crying, pacing.

10/9/37 Weight 143 lbs. Eat and sleeps well. Not so depressed. Is gradually showing improvement. Quiet and relevant.

6/23/38 Weight 156 lbs. Eats and sleeps well. Good weight gain. In good physical condition. Remains reclusive, but not as agitated as on admission.

9/4/38 Patient walked outside today. Continues to be noncommunicative with staff, 'talks' to non-present family members.

10/10/38 Patient observed watching train, nodding as though counting cars.

3/13/39 Patient brought in today by an employee, picked up on side of road near Waterloo. Says he thought he could leave as long as he was back by evening.

4/7/39 Continues to show interest in train visible from north grounds. Good appetite.

5/1/36 Patient walking outside today, singing "Jesus Loves Me."

5/25/39 Weight 175. Has been planting corn with farm crew. No signs of depression. Is greatly improved mentally at this time and appears to be his normal self.

6/1/39 Patient escaped today, law enforcement notified.

Reuben's Journal, 1936 – 1939

Entry 1

I'm sorry Daddy
I'm sorry Baby Girl
I'm sorry Laura
I failed
I did wrong
I failed
I didn't save money
I lost my money
I didn't provide for my family
I love my family
I failed
My mind is wrong
I fear for my soul
I should die
Somebody kill me
Bury me
I want to die

Entry 2

Little girl
I held dandelions
Under your chin
Sang "You are my Sunshine"
Oh, baby girl
Your daddy misses you
My sunshine is gone
My life is a dark cloud
I should die
I failed my baby girl

Entry 3

dank and dark this room
state-issued green
I wrap arms around knees
rock

plan, I have to get out
I will get out
I'm smart

I hide pills
under my tongue
I watch
for an unlocked door
I listen
for that train

I wait

Entry 4

Daddy told me
Jesus loves me
Nothing can separate
Me from the Love
of Jesus
Help me Jesus

Baby girl
I love you
I can't come back
I'm leaving and
I can't come back
Understand
Life is precious
in His hands
Daddy told me

Baby girl
you have angels
all around you
Daddy told me

Reuben's Journals, 1939 - 1950

Under a New Leaf

June 6, 1939 – November, 1943

Waterloo, Iowa
Austin, Minnesota
Wrenshall, Minnesota
Britt, Iowa
Dixon, Illinois
Lincoln, Illinois
Springfield, Illinois
St. Louis, Missouri
Carbondale, Illinois
Anna, Illinois
Cobden, Illinois

The Anna to Santa Fe Trail

November, 1943 – January, 1947

Karnak, Illinois
Cairo, Illinois
Memphis, Tennessee
Natchez, Mississippi
New Orleans, Louisiana
Tuscaloosa, Alabama
Lincoln, Illinois
Belle Plaine, Iowa
Britt, Iowa
Pawhuska, Oklahoma
Cherokee, Oklahoma
Guymon, Oklahoma
Boise City, Oklahoma
Clayton, New Mexico
Gladstone, New Mexico
Farley, New Mexico
Santa Fe, New Mexico
Cochiti, New Mexico

Under a New Leaf

"Path of logic, path of folly, all
The same—and I stand, my face lifted now skyward..." Robert Penn Warren, *Heart of Autumn*

WATERLOO, IOWA

June 1, 1939

collar up, hat down
into the light
someone who wasn't and now is

grasp the side bar—
jump moving train

don't look back

I'm free

AUSTIN, MINNESOTA

June 24, 1939

Oh God, what have I done?

June 26, 1939

In an abandoned outhouse, hiding from a storm from hell. Stink covers me like a heavy blanket and the wind screams at me to die. I get out my journal and think of nothing but moving this pencil across a new page. Again and again, I breathe.

June 27, 1939

I never thought I'd get so hungry I'd dig through trash or steal eggs and eat them raw. But here I am starving and filthy, hiding in shadows, waiting for darkness to kill me.

June 30, 1939

Things are looking up. I walked into Austin and asked around for a job. Maybe life is good after all. Not only do I have work making a dollar a day, but I have a bed in the barn and a noon-day meal, too.

Dorene, I think I'm going to make it.

August 14, 1939

nothing so pleasurable
as morning fog
in corn field shucked and cleaned

Oh Dorene, some days I could dance. The meadow lark's song as bright as sunshine.

But most days, I miss you so much, the daughter I left behind. I barely put one foot in front of the other. I have no joy in living.

From first pay, I bought a comb, hair cream, nail clippers, and a pocket calendar.

September 4, 1939

Alone with my journal. Thinking of my little girl, thinking about my life.

Sometimes I have to stop writing.

September 7, 1939

Library, looked up the word 'hobo' in the dictionary. Comes from "hoe boy" or a farm worker who travels looking for work, food, and lodging. I need to keep moving, and I'm best at farm work.

A hobo's life for me.

September 14, 1939

A dog's day in September, still warm enough to be outside. I've spent the afternoon fishing and pondering the path that's brought me here, where I've been and why things happen the way they do.

It was all the noise that pushed me over the edge, into that darkness of soul where I hear voices. Yelling they're going to kill me. I can't think, rest my mind, or write. I get so, so tired, and something inside me screams, and I want to die.

But somehow, here I am, still living; I've got hope in a new start.

Now if I could just catch some fish.

September 16, 1939 My 40th Birthday.

I've run out of luck, walked from farm to farm and no work. Went to a hobo jungle for a can of hot soup and heard talk about the lumber mills north of here. Maybe it's time to move on.

Jumped the Soo Line to Duluth.

WRENSHALL, MINNESOTA

September 18, 1939

Got a job on a dairy farm between Carlton and Wrenshall. Hired for farm chores, cutting trees, hauling logs, burning brush. I get a corner in the barn with a heating stove, two meals, and 50 cents a day. Surrounded by white pine forest.

Life is good.

September 19, 1939

Hauled milk to depo—five 10-gallon cans. Fixed Mr. Lehman's hay stack, wrapped wire around it so wouldn't blow off again. Went to Wrenshall, bought long underwear and a sock cap.

October 24, 1939

I haven't heard the voices in a long time. Maybe they're finally going to leave me alone.

November 11, 1939

Blizzard through the night, drifts over 20 feet in some places. Staying in barn until I can shovel my way out.

The voices are back, screaming at me. I cover my ears, but they're inside of me, like razorblades slicing through me. Oh God, oh God, oh God, help me.

Jumped out of hay window, only about a 6-foot drop with all the snow. Went to Lehman's house, the voices quiet there.

November 23, 1939 Thanksgiving Day

Dan Lehman brought a plate of Thanksgiving feast to the barn. A lot I should be thankful for, but when I'm here by myself, alone with my memories, I remember who I am. Would they be so good to me, if they knew – I escaped from the crazy house with a daughter who wonders where her daddy is and a wife who's glad he's gone?

December 18, 1939

At school Christmas program. George Lehman recited Robert Frost's "Stopping by Woods on a Snowy Evening." I especially enjoyed the ending "*…but I have promises to keep, and miles to go before I sleep, and miles to go before I sleep.*" When I got back to the barn, I started practicing it myself.

December 25, 1939 Christmas Day

Cleaned the Lehman's barn. Took a basket of Mrs. Lehman's pies and breads around to some neighbors. A family of Greeks invited me inside to warm up, gave me a jug of cider and a dessert they call baklava to take back to the Lehman's.

This evening, I'm sitting on a milk can in a freshly cleaned barn, with a plate of ham, mashed potatoes and gravy, bread warm from the oven, pumpkin pie, and some of that baklava. It's a fine day.

January 1, 1940

One of the Greeks stopped by with a sack full of paperback westerns. The Lehman's invited us for New Year's supper, fried squirrel with beans and cornbread.

January 6, 1940

Snow so icy and slick, took about two hours just to get the cows in the barn. Grateful for the coat and gloves from Mr. Lehman, and the hot soup and warm-from-the-oven from his wife. I don't deserve people like this.

January 10, 1940

Dark day, alone, and I want to die. I *should* die. God, just let me die.

January 16, 1940   Dorene's Birthday

I remember holding a dandelion under your chin while I sang "You are my Sunshine."

Painful memories.

January 18, 1940   Hildur's Birthday

I always loved your name, Hildur Astrid Martinson, like the name for a flower, dark and beautiful. You're 34 today.

Mr. Lehman sent me to Carlton to get the spring wagon fixed.

On bench outside barber shop. someone left a newspaper with a headline about a "blockbuster" movie, *The Invisible Man*. It gives me chills, a voice without a body, killing and terrorizing people—why would anyone with a right mind want to watch it?

February 2, 1940 Groundhog Day

"If you want to know what the weather will be, look at a pine cone. They open in good weather and close when storms are on the way." (*Farmer's Almanac,* 1940)

February 12, 1940

A man was shot in the forehead and killed in Wrenshall today. It should have been me - somebody should just kill me and get it over with.

February 21, 1940

When they came to arrest me, they said it was for desertion of minor children. I was trying to find work, walking miles every day. There was no work to be found. So, the kids are better off if I'm in jail? How's that for desertion?

They arrested me on November 9, 1936. I spent 2 weeks in Vinton city jail, treated like a dog. It'd make anybody crazy. I couldn't take it, couldn't sleep, started hearing voices. They wanted to kill me, said I didn't deserve to live. I started crying and couldn't stop. They hauled me off to the state hospital where I stayed for three years and couldn't take that either, locked in my room most of the time or watched like a hawk. If I'm proud of anything, it's that I got away from there.

March 24, 1940 Easter Sunday

Jacob oil for a toothache.

April 10, 1940

Dan Lehman brought a newspaper from Wrenshall. Headline: Germany has invaded Norway. Everyone's worrying about the war coming here. Who's going to stop it?

May 2, 1940

George Lehman showed me how to roll a wheel with a stick.

May 10, 1940

Hitler has invaded France, and I'm at the library, reading *Collected Poems* by Mark Van Doren. *"After long drought, commotion in the sky: after dead silence, thunder. Then it comes..."* And then it comes, evil, cold, and deadly. God help us all.

May 12, 1940 Mother's Day

I can never have a Mother's Day without pain. Mother died when I was 7. The world went dark and I stayed in bed until one of my aunts came and sat beside me and told me to be brave, Mother would want me to be brave; I've tried, but I don't remember a day since without melancholy.

It's my fault Mama died; I got sick first, then she got sick caring for me. Father blamed me too.

My mother's name was Anna Matilda, but everyone called her Tillie. Her parents were Anna and Peter Janson. I don't remember my grandfather, but I called Anna the Swedish word for grandmother—Mormor. She was a good woman, stood straight-backed. A hard-working woman who expected her children to behave and work hard, too. I loved her.

May 21, 1940 Laura's Birthday

We were married when I was 33, and Laura was 28, a widow with 4 young boys. Maybe she was desperate for a husband and help with her children, or maybe she really loved me.

Planted a half-acre of potatoes for Mrs. Lehman. She sent a plate of cookies to the barn for me. Dan said they're called Cry Baby Cookies, said his mom's about famous for them. I can see why.

May 22, 1940

I thanked Mrs. Lehman for the cookies, told her they were delicious, and asked how she made them. She recited the recipe from memory.

Cry Baby Cookies

1 cup shortening
1 cup sugar
1 cup molasses
2 eggs
4 ½ cup flour
2 teaspoons cinnamon
2 teaspoons ginger
½ teaspoon salt
2 teaspoons baking soda
1 cup raisins
1 cup nuts, chopped
1 cup hot coffee

Mix and bake on greased cookie sheets in a 350° oven, about 8 minutes.

June 1, 1940

Helped Mrs. Lehman plant cabbages and tomatoes. After supper, Mrs. Lehman killed a porcupine in her garden with one shot.

June 8, 1940

Ball game in Wrenshall with Dan Lehman. Most fun I can remember. I forgot my pain, hoping for a home run.

June 16, 1940 Father's Day

A sad day, Mr. Lehman passed away. He wasn't feeling well, but wouldn't see a doctor. Said if it was his time to go, he was ready.

June 19, 1940

Funeral for Mr. Lehman

I sit with my journal and watch the sun go down.

June 21, 1940

The Lehman's are moving to Illinois; one of their sons has a farm in Jordan Township. Mrs. Deison says she never wanted to live in Minnesota anyway, and the Greeks have offered to rent their farm, so there's no reason to stay.

They gave me the address and invited me to stop by anytime.

June 23, 1940

Time for me to move on. Went to a jungle in Duluth and heard about a hobo convention in Britt, Iowa, just south of Minnesota border. Sounds like something to check out.

BRITT, IOWA

August, 2 1940

Hitchhiked to Britt, good food, good friends, good time. Met folks that felt like family.

Hobos come from across the Unites States to gather beside a rusted water tower on the edge of town. Farmers donate produce, bakers share day-old bread, stew is boiled in barrels over open fires—a celebration of life on the road and rail.

August 3, 1940

After breakfast, a woman wearing bib overalls and a red bandana jumped up on a platform, and called with a loud voice, "Welcome to our jungle, a home for hungry travelers, and a resting place for weary souls. I'm Connecticut Red, one of the organizers of this event. Our mulligan stew is the best you'll taste, folks adding to it all day. Our current batch is squirrel, sausage, tomatoes, and potatoes. The recipe changes by the hour!"

August 4, 1940

We had a ceremony this morning. I am officially a hobo, having sworn the Hobo's Oath for all to hear:

> "I solemnly swear to do all in my power to aid and assist all those willing to aid and assist themselves, I pledge myself to assist all runaway boys and girls and induce them to return to their homes and parents. So help me God."

My new name is Dakota Swede.

I was given a paper with signs to look for on box cars, trees, and fence posts, drawn by other hobos, where to find food, and when to leave in a hurry.

I learned the difference between hobos, tramps, and bums—hoboes will work, tramps won't, and bums can't. I will work, but there are other things I'd rather do instead.

August 5, 1940

Have decided to stay in Iowa for a while. Plenty of farm work this time of year.

Made a bed with my jacket under a tree.

August 7, 1940

All the farms around are fenced. I finally found one with an open gate. Unfortunately, their dog wasn't welcoming strangers and took a bite out of my pants as I was leaving.

August12, 1940

Shocked wheat for a dollar and lunch.

August 19. 1940

I'm sleeping in an old box car in Britt's jungle. Most everyone's left and gone on to somewhere else. I'm enjoying being back in Iowa, in a town where no one knows me or cares who I am. I've missed the corn fields and August air.

Someone left an old bicycle. I patched the tires and am using it to ride around the county looking for work. Plenty of gardens to weed and potatoes to dig.

August 27, 1940

Saw a sign for Shank Farms, and underneath the sign someone had carved two shovels, which meant there was work there. I followed the lane to the farmhouse and knocked on the door. A woman who looks so much like Laura, I had to look twice, said, "Hello, can I help you?"

When I asked if she had any work I could do, she said her husband was harvesting corn and could probably use an extra hand. She pointed to a big field behind the barn and told me I'd find him there.

To make a long story short, I've got a good week-long job, helping with corn harvest.

August 31, 1941

Sitting on back steps eating breakfast when a young boy came running into the yard yelling, "Help, my daddy's tractor turned over on him, and I can't get him out!" I called Mr. Shank, and he came running with his two boys.

"He's in a ditch on Hutchins Road. He's hurt bad!" Then the boy started crying, and Mr. Shank told him not to worry. He'd call the rescue squad in Britt and then he'd go see what he could do, make sure the tractor was turned off, and nothing was leaking. "I might be able to pull it off with my truck or jack it up enough to get him out from under it."

I offered to go along. I don't know what I thought I could do, but I couldn't just sit there and go on with my breakfast.

The man was screaming when we got there, the bottom half of his body pinned beneath the big rear tire. We worked as fast as we could to jack it up and slide him out, but I could tell with one look, the man wasn't going to walk again.

An ambulance came and got him, and I wasn't worth much the rest of the day.

September 3, 1940

Depression grabs me by the heart and pulls me deeper and deeper down into bottomless blackness.

September 5, 1940

Back at the Shanks to see if I could work for food. Spent the morning cutting dead flowers, piling and burning brush. Lunch on the porch, I watch their granddaughter in pigtails chasing her kittens, her laughter fills the air like music. Oh Dorene, you'll never know how much I miss you.

She came up to me later and held out a small twig. "See my fat caterpillar? He's got lots of fur to keep him warm."

"Indeed he does," I said and looked away so she wouldn't see the tear rolling down my face.

September 9, 1940

The Shanks haven't offered me a place to stay, and the boxcar's getting chilly. I can either get moving or sit here 'til I die.

Sep 10, 1940

dreaming of places I've heard of
but never thought I'd see –

first footsteps in fresh snow
I'm heading South

DIXON, ILLINOIS

September 14, 1940

Hopped off when train slowed near Dixon—found a gathering of hobos by the water tower. First thing I did was head for the mulligan, not too bad. After my second tin can-full, I asked where the work was. (Decided I'd wait for spring to find farm work.) Turns out this town has two fine hotels that will give you a bed, food, and fifty cents a day, for kitchen help and housekeeping.

There's also a YMCA – went there next to clean up, then straight to the Morrison Hotel, and would you believe, I had a job within 10 minutes.

I believe if a man makes himself presentable and isn't above cleaning spittoons and toilets, and he'll almost always find work.

September 16, 1940 My Birthday

The Selective Service Act passed today, the draft – requiring all men between the ages of 21 – 35 to register. I'm glad I'm too old, how could I register and have the government know where I am? I failed my family. I might as well fail my country too.

October 12, 1940

Afternoon off, I found the library to check newspapers for news about the war. More of the same, bombings, invasions, people dying. I'm tired of the war, and I'm not even fighting, just tired of hearing about it, tired of worrying about it, tired of seeing the screaming, dying bodies when I close my eyes at night.

Went to the history room and looked up Jordan Township (where the Lehmans moved) and read about Buffalo Creek Valley, Chief Black Hawk, and a ghost town called Berwick. The author called the area 'pristine'. I believe I hear it calling my name.

I wrote a letter to the Lehmans, letting them know I was in Dixon, gave them my address at Morrison Hotel.

October 28, 1940

All this talk about the election, I'll be glad when it's over. There's nothing wrong with Wilkie, but we're in a war and standing strong under Roosevelt. Even if it is his third term, this country's behind him.

Got a letter from Dan Lehman inviting me to come.

November 5, 1940

Presidential election – Roosevelt won.

December 24, 1940

Remembering my childhood tonight. It wasn't easy. Didn't matter if it was twenty below, I fed and milked the cows, slopped hogs, and tended horses every morning before school–and every Saturday, no matter if it was Christmas, I cleaned the barn.

Hildur took care of the carriage horse and chickens, and worked like a man in the fields.

Even if we had to work hard, Christmas was a special time. Father made lutefisk from dried fish shipped from Norway. The first week in December, he'd bring the wooden tub up from the basement and set it on the back porch. Then he'd soak the fish in a mix of lye and water for about three weeks. On Christmas Eve day, he'd make cream and mustard gravies and melted butter to serve with it.

Aunt Elsa, Father's sister, would make her seven kinds of cookies. First was the pepper kakor, like a ginger cookie. Delicious. We children got all the burned and broken ones so we tried to be around the kitchen on her baking days.

A big get-together Christmas Eve, all the aunts, uncles, and cousins. We decorated a tree with candles. Around 11:00 at night, the candles were lit, and our holiday smorgasbord would be ready. In addition to lutefisk, we had coffee cakes, head cheese, pickled pigs' feet, pickled herring, rye bread—too many things to remember. We gave our gifts to each other after that.

Dinner was served by candlelight. The table was fancy with polished silverware and china from Sweden on a white linen cloth.

After the feast, Father would open the doors to show our Christmas tree in all its glory. He'd sit beside the tree and read the Christmas story from the Bible. Then we'd all sing together old carols and have a happy time.

December 25, 1940

Here I am alone in a hotel basement on Christmas day. Piles of dirty towels and sheets instead of holiday decorations, and a plate of yesterday's leftovers for my feast. I should kill myself and get it over with.

December 29, 1940

Listening to one of FDR's Fireside Chats – he says our country is a leader in the free world, and we have a responsibility to supply our allies with weapons. He called the United States the 'arsenal of democracy' and has issued a call to arms.

A cold hand squeezes my heart.

January 16, 1941 Dorene's Birthday

Your birthday, you're eight years old today. Hope it's a happy day for you, and you remember happy times. In your memory, that's what I'll do, too.

I remember the day you were born, maybe the happiest day of my life. Laura and I were on our way back from visiting family in North Dakota. We got as far as St. Paul, and she said Reuben, I think the baby's coming. You were born that evening, at Lutheran Hospital.

I chose your name, Dorene, because it has strong and solid sound, and Mae, because I think May is the prettiest month of the year. Dorene Mae Martinson, how glad I was to meet you.

I never thought I'd be spending my life without you.

January 18, 1941 Hildur's Birthday

Father made sure we had a piano for Hildur to take lessons. I didn't like her music teacher much, slapping her hands with a ruler when she made a mistake, but Father didn't seem to notice, and Hildur loved playing, and would practice for hours.

January 20, 1941

President Roosevelt inaugurated for third term. Heated discussion in the jungle. Some say he's prolonging the war, demanding unconditional surrenders. Others complained about his New Deal and how it's not working. I stay out of it.

February 4, 1941

Darn groundhog

February 23, 1941

Gave Mr. Morrison notice I'd be leaving when the weather warms up. Hotel work is fine for getting through the cold winter, but when the weather warms up, I want to be outside.

April 12, 1941

Finally, it's spring! Heading out to the Lehmans.

Mrs. Lehman glad to see me. Dan took me around the neighborhood, letting everyone know an extra hired hand was available.

A farmer named Warner Diller hired me full time, $3.00 a day and I can sleep in the hay loft.

Some of the most beautiful countryside I've ever imagined. I see why Black Hawk came back every year.

April 13, 1941

Helped Mrs. Lehman plant green beans and sweet corn.

April 15, 1941

Helped Shorty Morrison castrate hogs – it's his father who has hotel in Dixon – small world. Was invited to supper, fried mountain oysters, mashed potatoes, green beans, and cherry pie.

Morrison daughters are like stair steps, six girls towheaded and tan. They must be part Swede. Twin baby girls; the oldest is about 12.

They invited me to spend the night, to sleep on the davenport. I didn't see a reason not to.

April 16, 1941

Mrs. Morrison and I got on the subject of nationality this morning. I told her I was Swede. She said she was half, her dad was Swede, her mom was German. I told her she had the hazel eyes and high cheekbones of a Swede, the height, too. She nodded and said she saw the Swede in me too.

May 10, 1941

Twirled jump rope with the Morrison girls this morning.

Mrs. Morrison gave me a haircut and wouldn't let me pay.

June 7, 1941

Helped Jane Diller plant sweet corn, beans, peas, tomatoes, lettuce, and beets.

June 21, 1941 Father's Day

Rode to Feed Store in Milledgeville with Shorty Morrison. He got such a kick out of telling me dirty jokes, I couldn't help laughing.

June 23, 1941

Found a spring with cold water for drinking and nice shade to sit and write.

sunny morning smell of forest—
is that why the birds are singing?

I can't be sad on a day this bright and blue.

June 25, 1941

Germany has invaded Russia. They're trying to take over the world, and someone has to stop them. I may not be a smart man, but I know cold-blooded and evil.

July 12, 1941

Mowed hayfields, then turned the hay to dry.

After a day in the fields, nothing refreshes like jumping in the creek.

September 9, 1941

Spent the morning picking up big rocks and stacking them along the fence row. This afternoon, planted winter wheat.

September, 11, 1941

Helped Lehmans with butchering. When I left, Mrs. Lehman gave me a bucket filled with fried chicken and biscuits.

She asked if I like to fish, said there were always good catfish in the Elkhorn. She said, "Be sure to throw a big rock in the creek before you go in – runs off the water moccasins."

September 13, 1941

nothing more glorious
sunlight on
September wheat

Fished today, cooking catfish on a stick over a campfire. I'm a thankful man.

I met Bishop Good from the Mennonite Church in Sterling at the Lehman's yesterday. He shook my hand and invited me to Sunday service and picnic afterward. I never turn down a meal.

September 14, 1941

Science Ridge Mennonite Church – during the service, Bishop looked right at me and said, "Therefore welcome one another as Christ has welcomed you, to the glory of God."

September 16, 1941 My 42nd Birthday

Just another day, I haven't told anyone it's my birthday—who cares?

September 17, 1941

Tragedy in the neighborhood. The oldest Deyo boy dropped his loaded shot gun and accidently shot his mother in the face. She's not expected to live, leaving behind eleven children. The boy has run away, said he was changing his name and moving to California.

Mr. Morrison invited me to supper. Beef & noodles, green beans from garden, apricot pie like Laura used to make.

I follow cow path
to familiar spot
thick tree branch
across stream

I sit cool in shade
and think of you

October 10, 1941

Finished plowing. Spent rest of day digging turnips.

November 19, 1941

A full day working for Mr. Diller, spread manure and harrowed it in, cleaned garden, burned weeds and rubbish. Tomorrow he's sending me to Lehmans to help make casings for sausage. Glad to be busy—when I'm working, the voices are quiet.

December 7, 1941

Japanese warplanes have attacked Pearl Harbor— 2500 people killed without warning.

I have no words.

December 8, 1941

I record this date as the beginning of a world war. President Roosevelt has officially declared war against Japan. Something is squeezing me by the throat. I have to write about something else.

Going for a walk.

December 11, 1941

Now Germany and Italy have declared war on the United States. I can't eat or sleep. Voices shout in my ears. God help us all.

December 14, 1941

I haven't left the barn in three days. I might as well die and get it over with.

December 15, 1941

Oscar came by today and saw me in the clothes I've slept in for a week; my hair not combed for that long either. He acted like he didn't notice and told me that the neighborhood kids were meeting at the top of the hill outside this barn. He wanted to warn me about the noise. Then he grinned and said, "Extra sled's in the corn crib if you want to join them."

When I heard all the shouting, I started watching from the barn. The more I watched, the more I wanted to feel that, sliding as far and fast as I could down a long steep hill.

Finally, I thought what the heck, cleaned myself up, went out and took turn after turn, with nothing on my mind but icy wind and speed.

Those voices haven't killed me yet.

December 17, 1941

Helped Lehman brothers with butchering.

December 25, 1941 Christmas Day

I remember my last St. Lucia Day at home, Hildur was about 11. She got up before the rest of us, like she did every year, and made Lucia buns. Then she put on a white robe with a red sash around her waist. She wore a crown of pine with five candles and brought us the buns on a tray, singing *Santa Lucia* like an angel. She was so beautiful.

Father said the name Lucia means 'light", and St. Lucia Day, a celebration of the light which came into the world when Christ was born. It was the official start of our Christmas.

The next two weeks were busy with cooking, cleaning, and making gifts.

LINCOLN, ILLINOIS

January 1, 1942

I've had it with winter, freezing my you-know-what off. Like the geese did weeks ago, I'm heading south.

Hitchhiked from Rock Island to Lincoln, sleeping in a barn again. Thank God for small favors.

Everyone's pockets are empty.

Oh-la-la, I've heard of Cherry Pie Nellie from Lincoln, but this pie is something else. I think she's got a soft spot for me – she fixed me a lunch bucket, cold bean soup and a fried potato sandwich, fine eating. I offered to come back tomorrow and fix her porch step.

January 2, 1942

When I got to Cherry's this morning. there was a jar of ginger tea and a piece of sweet potato pie sitting on the table outside her door.

We sat on her porch this evening. She sure does enjoy a good visit. I think she told me a little about everything she knows. She called herself a pow-wow doctor—uses natural remedies to help with all sorts of things. One thing she said that stuck with me—a tea made from borage flowers is good for melancholy.

She asked me about myself—I told her I was a traveling farm worker who liked writing and sharing poetry. I recited for her one of my favorites I wrote about Carl Sandburg. She was impressed and said I have the voice of a poet.

She says someday my ship will come in, whatever that means.

Carl and I

I read Carl Sandburg
and wonder, are we related?
free spirits, tender souls
full of northern prairie
sun and sky

color words
red heart
silver moon
blue rain
tint our
bond of life

wanderer, comrade
fellow dreamer
paint my fog
with cat's feet

Swedish American
me too
hobo heart
me too

January 3, 1942

Think I'll spend another day working on Miss Cherry's porch, see if she has anything else I can do.

Laura doesn't need to know everything.

SPRINGFIELD, ILLINOIS

January 5, 1942

Thanks to Cherry, I left Lincoln with a full stomach, new haircut, a flour sack filled with ham sandwiches and cookies—and an invitation to stop by anytime I'm in Lincoln.

Walking 6th Street

morning walk
in Springfield
   heart of
   Illinois
before sounds of
city rush
fill the air

stately structures
painted pillars
dated stones

this street
strolled for a century
   and decades more

politicians
lawyers, lawmen
bankers, clerks
window washers
street sweepers
   young Abe

and wonder-struck
farm boys
   such as I

Found a flop house and tell myself this is just temporary.

January 10, 1942

The guy on the cot next to me told me that the Lake House Nightclub was looking for help in the kitchen, said it was the "hottest" spot in town. People come from all over, well-known entertainers like Bob

Hope, Mickey Rooney, Guy Lombardo. Sounded like it was worth a try.

Was hired on the spot. Dishwasher for 20 cents an hour and all the leftovers I want. Music was an added bonus. When the dishes were done for the night, I took advantage of the raised dance floor and danced for the first time in years.

Didn't realize it was a gambling hot-spot as well. Police raided, and I left through the back door.

ST. LOUIS, MISSOURI

January 13, 1942

My clothes are dirty and ragged, and Cherry's food is gone. Found a jungle and asked about a mission so here I am, in a flop house again, on a cot in a room with about 30 other strangers and misfits, a belly full of thin soup and stale bread, and a hole in my heart the size of Boston.

January 14, 1942

Went to the mission store this morning, I found a good Sunday suit, shoes, and a book of poems by Robert Frost.

The title of the book is 'In the Clearing,' perfect name for it. These poems take me with them. Here's one with something to think about. I've read it ten times at least.

Spirit enters flesh
And for all it's worth
Charges into earth
In birth after birth

I also got a pocket New Testament. I'll carry it over my heart.

January 15, 1942

"Wouldn't you rather be mopping?" is the new slogan in the flop house. Translation: cleaning a floor is better than lying around with your hand out.

My pride is gone, and I'm an empty shell, standing in line at the relief office, waiting for my small bit of government assistance. God, get me out of this.

Brother McCormick at the mission talks about 'rejoicing in our sufferings.' Doesn't seem possible. Suffering is darn suffering.

I had to scratch out yesterday's writing—lost my temper and used words I don't want anyone to read.

Darn dark ugly life. Some days I want to die.

Walked out to the jungle to hear what was going on, talk to people. Decided I've been spending too much time alone. There was talk about southern Illinois and all the work there, orchards, produce farms, and a milder winter. That part got my attention.

In the jungle, a gray-haired hobo using a crate for a stage, gave one of the best performances of Shakespeare I've ever seen. I stayed until he was through, then went up and shook his hand, told him how much I enjoyed the show. I didn't catch his name, Texas Jim or something like that. He thanked me and invited me to stay for his comedy act. So funny I laughed out loud—something about a man giving flowers to all his girlfriends, then forgetting which ones he gave to who.

He gave me a poem, said it was mine.

Waiting for Life to Unfold

I watch them pass.
Floating leaf blankets
springing flowers
as they flee winter.

Yesterday's blues
dissolve unwanted memories;
and randomly align in my stream
of good intentions.

Tomorrow will gently rock
the next flotilla

as I await
the last tide.

January 16, 1942 Dorene's Birthday

So many times, I'd take you in the stroller to get some quiet. We'd walk to the railroad tracks south of Luzerne where we lived, and count the cars together, especially enjoying the long trains. You got so you could count to twelve by yourself and were so happy about it, you'd count the numbers one through twelve over and over until the train finally ended, then wave at the caboose.

And you loved singing nursery rhymes. We sang hundreds together, and you loved every one. I think your favorite was "Mares Eat Oats." I'll never forget the sound of your voice. *"Mares eat oats and does eat oats, and little lambs eat ivy. A kid'll eat ivy too, wouldn't you?"* Tears roll down my face remembering, bouncing you on my lap, singing it again and again. Before I left you could sing it by yourself.

January 18, 1942 Hildur's Birthday

My sister Hildur always seemed so sad, except when she was galloping bareback. I can see her now, chestnut hair blowing behind her, face against the wind.

February 3, 1942

Snowed-in in St. Louis
Darn this weather

I know I should be glad for this cot, this rag of a blanket, hot broth and old coffee, and at least there's heat— but this is not living, this is slow dying.

I can hear voices in the blizzard. Most of the time, the voices muffle, and I can't understand. But today they're clear as crystal. Am I the only one who hears them? Am I really so darn worthless I should die?

February 9, 1942

We lived next door to Laura's parents, which was part of the problem. Her father was against me from the start. He called me a bum, not good enough for his daughter. He was right.

February 23, 1942

At least the flop house has a radio. Everyone is listening to President Roosevelt's Fireside Chat about the progress of the war. He's trying to cheer everybody up, "Don't worry, we'll work together and win this thing." Mr. President, I hope you're right.

March 13, 1942

Talk at the mission about southern Illinois, calling it Little Egypt. Brother McCormick told about a severe winter in 1830, followed by a late spring – not much corn planted north of Jefferson County. Then an early frost in 1831 completely ruined all corn north of Carlyle. South of Carlyle, the corn crop was abundant. People from northern Illinois traveled to southern Illinois to buy corn and were reminded of the Bible story about the sons of Jacob going down to Egypt for corn. So the southern tip of Illinois has been called Little Egypt ever since.

Little Egypt, here I come.

March 14, 1942

Since I'm leaving tomorrow, went looking for a day's work and a little extra travel money. Not far out of town, I found a well-kept farm and asked for odd jobs. Well, not only did the farmer have a harness that needed repaired, he had apple trees to whitewash as well.

I now have two dollars; I'm heading to the Promised Land.

The train whistle calls me.

CARBONDALE, ILLINOIS

March 16, 1942

Caught a freight train out of St. Louis – jumped off when it slowed for Carbondale. Man in the jungle told me Arnold's Orchards was hiring, south of town. Went to a service station and cleaned up, combed my hair, then headed to Arnold's.

God might be smiling on me after all. Not only did I get a job, but a little room off the barn, too, with a straw bed and kerosene stove – what more could a man want.

day of new beginnings
sunshine on daffodils

April 1, 1942

Well, little girl, it's a fine day isn't it – first buttercups of spring.

cold green
mossy rocks
drip with winter melt

April 18, 1942 Palm Sunday

I was confirmed on Palm Sunday, when I was fourteen. We had a family feast, a smorgasbord of Swedish cooking at its best.

The Saturday before Easter, Father would go around and pick up the kids in the neighborhood, making several trips in his wagon—he'd hide dozens of boiled eggs, and give each child a basket with a cardboard egg filled with chocolate. After all the eggs were found, we'd have a picnic of eggs, ham sandwiches, and Aunt Mary's family-famous cookies. One of the happiest days of the year.

On Easter Sunday, we'd come home after church for a big gathering and another smorgasbord. Mormor had her specialty, potato and anchovy stew. And Father always roasted a leg of lamb.

I remember Hildur delighted in decorating the house—she collected birch twigs and tied colored feathers on each. She put vases of them all around the house.

April 25, 1942 Easter Sunday

I think Dutchman's breeches are my favorite. They look like white knee pants, hung on a green line.

I'll never forget the Easter after the terrible accident, when we lost Nell, Hildur's carriage horse. We were short a work horse and decided to use Nell. She spooked about something, reared back and fell into the harrow, and was stabbed by about a dozen six-inch blades. A bloody sight, with Nell screaming and kicking her legs as we stood watching, unable to help.

Our Easter was a painful and empty holiday that year; no decorating, no egg hunt or party. The aunts brought food but a sad silence covered the meal.

Hildur didn't talk for about two weeks.

May 10, 1942 Mother's Day

When I think of Mother, I think of spice cookies. I loved helping her, the way the kitchen smelled, and the laughter in her voice. Father accused me of being a "mama's boy" but I didn't care. I was happy to be my mother's son.

Mother and Father came to America in 1885; they met on the boat on the way over from Sweden, Father traveling from Skőne, and Mother from Stockholm. They were married at the Swedish Lutheran Church in Hample, North Dakota. Laura has their pictures.

June 21, 1942

I'm sorry, Father, I failed. I shirked my work and failed my family. Why can't I just die?

June 23, 1942

I watch a family of bluebirds flutter against the wind, and think of you, Dorene.

August 25, 1942

Taking a break from threshing to cool my feet in the stream, write my thoughts to you, my daughter, my precious Dorene. Sometimes I pretend you're here with me, and sometimes I forget I'm pretending.

September 16, 1942 My 43rd Birthday

I don't know what to think about the war, I hear about thousands of Jews being killed for no reason except they're Jews. Is that what this war is about? I thought it was about getting back at Japan and helping our allies. You sure can't believe anything you hear.

November 17, 1942

Mr. Arnold's run out of work for me. He thanked me for being a trustworthy worker, gave me a leather satchel he said he wasn't going to need again. He told me about a friend with a large farm near Nashville and wrote down his name and directions.

Now tonight I find a train ticket to Nashville in the satchel, and I see Mrs. Arnold put in some biscuits and ham.

Before I leave, I'm going to look around a bit – I've heard there's plenty of work and winter's mild enough. Mr. Arnold doesn't have the only orchard in southern Illinois, and that ticket will keep.

November 18, 1942

Didn't get far. Walked south about five miles and found a place so peaceful, I didn't want to leave. Made a lean-to out of a canvas Mr. Arnold gave me, next to a bluff with a stream nearby. Newspapers on pine needles make a fine bed, and it's warm enough beside a fire. Moon so bright I can write by it.

I've heard there's good work around Anna – several farms and a bakery.

November 19, 1942

light explodes   sunrise on frozen river

Took some time this morning to explore. This sure is pretty country. Plenty of time to get to Nashville.

Have discovered a community nearby called Boskeydell, with a whistle stop. Good information to have.

November 20, 1942

Walked to Boskeydell, noticed a man chopping wood. I introduced myself and told him I was willing to work for food. He gave me the once over, then handed me his ax.

I chopped wood for a good two hours and laid the pile out in a circle, like Swedes do. The man was impressed. Shook my hand and introduced himself as Bill Curry. He had his wife fix me a gunny sack of bread and boiled potatoes. Then he noticed we were about the same size and offered me a Sunday suit and a pair of loafers, too. I'm set to meet the world.

He asked where I was staying—I described the location of my camp, and he said I picked a good spot.

I love the sound
a creek rock makes
as I cross to the other side

November 21, 1942 Our Anniversary

Laura and I were married on November 21, 1931, in her parents' home in Luzerne, Iowa. I think of us dancing on our wedding night, just the two of us. A happy time.

Father died three weeks after our wedding from an abscessed tooth. Too stubborn to go to a dentist and then it was too late. We went to the funeral, Laura and me. I cried for Father, more than I ever imagined I would. I was glad to have Laura beside me.

November 22, 1942

Two girls visited my camp this morning, Mr. Curry's young daughters, looked to be about 10 and 12. The oldest said her name was Jan and her sister was Betty June, both cute as buttons, blue-eyed and blonde. Jan had a gift for me. She called it a hobo survival kit, a Prince Albert can with everything a hobo needs – needle and thread, safety pins, matches, even a string for fishing.

They wanted to hear some hobo stories, so I made up a few, and recited a couple poems too. They loved it— applauded after each one. It was so good to have company, and Dorene, you're almost their age. They asked if I had family, and I said No, and then didn't feel like stories or poems any more.

They asked for hobo names before they left. I told them they were Boskey Jan and Betty June Bug. Then they asked me if I had a hobo name. When I told them Dakota Swede, Jan shook my hand and said "Nice to meet you, Mr. Swede." Betty June gave me a little curtsey.

There's good in the world, Dorene.

November 23, 1942

Went by Mr. Curry's to see if I could work for my supper. He didn't have anything I could do but invited me to eat with them anyway. Ham with yams and biscuits. Without a doubt, Mrs. Curry can cook.

under an outcropping
I watch the rain
listen to big drops fall

so lonely
I cry with the rain

ANNA, ILLINOIS

November 24, 1942

Before I left camp, I carved my initials in the sandstone wall that I've slept beside the past week. I'm almost sorry to leave.

Walked into Anna through early morning mist and fog—very pleasant, rolling hills, fields, and forests. Wasn't hard to find Lewis Bakery (followed my nose), fine people. Said they weren't hiring, but if I'd take the two-day old bread to the families in shanty town, I could have all the bread I wanted. I don't miss an opportunity for food.

Mr. Lewis suggested I go to the newspaper office, check there for work. He said, "Ask for Mr. Tellor and tell him Jack sent you."

Mr. Tellor said they were hiring bell hops at the Anna Hotel. I got hired on the spot (wearing the suit Mr. Curry gave me.) For 50₵ a day with tips and a room in the basement, I'll be the one to 'hop to action' whenever someone rings a bell.

November 25, 1942

Shanty town is by the railroad tracks, one and two-room shacks with ragtag children running everywhere.

When I delivered bread today, I heard some children singing "Oats, Peas, Beans, and Barley Grow." Dorene, do you remember? We'd hold hands and sing and dance in a circle.

I have to confess, my precious daughter, I sang that song at least a dozen times tonight, alone in my room, holding you in my heart.

I will only remember good things today.

November 26, 1942 Thanksgiving Day

Thanksgiving. What am I thankful for? I'm not in jail, not locked up somewhere. I can walk and talk, and that's about it.

December 1, 1942

President Roosevelt has ordered nationwide gasoline rationing. Looks like I'll be doing more walking.

December 5, 1942

December moon is wrapped in silver

The morning woke slowly, darkness clinging damp and heavy.

milk white moon
soft as a winter morning's fog
   lingers to greet the dawn

December 24, 1942

Father built our house by hand. A big two-story with carved doorposts, colonnades, and two parlors. It was a fine home and solid.

December 25, 1942

No matter how late we stayed up on Christmas Eve, the next morning everyone was up before dawn for Julotta, a special service at church that started at 5:30 on the dot. The organist came early so music was playing while everyone arrived. Hundreds of candles were lit to welcome everyone as well. The minister stood in the doorway to greet and shake our hands. We'd have a 'julbord' at lunchtime, a buffet of cold fish, ham, bread, and cheese.

For two weeks after Christmas, friends and neighbors stopped by, and we made the rounds of home visits too.

I try to think it's ok, Christmas alone, no money, eating hard bread in a hotel basement, and it's cold, damp cold. I hate my life. God must hate me too.

January 16, 1943   Dorene's 10th Birthday

Dorene, I have no words, only the pain in missing you. Please, just be happy and don't think about me.

January 18, 1943 Hildur's Birthday

After Mother died, Mormor and Aunt Mary Ester came two or three times a week and spent the afternoon baking and cleaning. Then when Hildur got old enough to take over some of it, and they stopped coming so much. I'm pretty sure Hildur preferred bread-making and house cleaning to field work, but she did a good share of that too.

January 30, 1943

From *Farmer's Almanac*:

"For frostbite: keep feet in warm, not hot, water and let them thaw slowly. Too much heat will add to injury.

"Milking by hand, there are 340 squirts in one gallon of milk."

February 2, 1943

Groundhog definitely didn't see his shadow this morning. The winter gray of southern Illinois is getting to me. I feel like I'm being smothered with a wet wool blanket, heavy and dark and miserable.

February 9, 1943

Good news. The US beat the crap out Japan at Guadalcanal.

February 14, 1943

gray days follow
gray days

February 22, 1943

Got fired from my job today. A big shot woman accused me of mishandling her luggage and breaking a mirror. It didn't do any good to defend myself; I'm just a bellhop. I was told to get my things and leave, and the last of my pay would replace the 'lady's' mirror.

Time to look for farm work. I've had enough jumping when someone rings a bell. I've heard the Flamms over in Cobden (about 6 miles from here) are good people and pay a good wage.

COBDEN, ILLINOIS

February 24, 1943

Writing is my soul singing across the page.

Not only did I get hired, Mr. Flamm offered me a one-room house with a bed, coal heater, and sink. Compared to other places I've spent the night, this is living in luxury.

March 24, 1943

Sharpened tools, raked and burned old brush.

April 4, 1943

Oh, the glory of a spring day, with nothing to do but whatever I want.

I came upon a dozen deer
who stared blank-faced and frozen
I prayed peace to them
but they didn't listen

and leapt white-tailed into
early morning thicket

greetings, lone bird
I almost didn't see you
quiet in spring breeze
do you enjoy the forest
soak in its stillness
as much as I?

From *Farmer's Almanac,*

"When clouds appear like rocks and towers, the earth's refreshed by frequent showers."

April 10, 1943

Nothing so happy as the song of a chickadee.

Enjoyed making a scarecrow for Mrs. Flamm's garden, then one of the kids heard me talking to you, started laughing and telling the other kids. Mr. Flamm came out and shushed him, but the fun was gone.

Noticed spiders are spinning new webs—Aunt Elsa always said that was a sign of fair weather.

Sunday – chicken dinner, I showed the Flamm boys the agate marble in my pocket so they challenged me to a game. I let Leonard win the agate so now I think I have a friend for life.

May 1, 1943

May is my favorite month, almost summer, trees full
green, flowers vibrant. Nature sings in May.

Dorene, did you know, not everyone sees the man in the moon (I'm reading a *Farmer's Almanac.*) The Japanese see a rabbit, and the Ojibwa see a boy stealing two buckets of water.

Spaded Mrs. Flamm's garden spot.

May 21, 1943 Laura's Birthday

Laura Louise Rosette Peterman, I do love you.

May 30, 1943

Three acres of strawberries, well-strawed and in fine shape. At eleven o'clock on Memorial Day, I counted over 100 pickers in the patch.

June 1, 1943

What a peaceful place, sitting beside Hutchens Creek, listening to the water ripple against the rocks, a Sunday afternoon vacation with my journal.

I love summer ponds and lakes and slow-moving creeks—
no higher moment than this—time stops to hear the water sing.

I stared at my reflection for a while, wondering who I am and why I am. Suddenly I couldn't bear to look.

July 4, 1943

Train emptied out at Makanda station for 4th of July celebration. Tables of food, platforms with politicians, and games for children—I joined in the gunny sack races; felt good to laugh out loud.

July 6, 1943

Laura, I'm sorry, so sorry, but I couldn't live with all the noise, all the arguing and yelling. You see what it did to me, where I ended up. I can't go back there, even if my heart is torn to shreds by leaving you and Dorene. Especially Dorene. I can still see her looking at me with so much love in her eyes. I can barely put one foot in front of the other.

Your boys knew I wasn't their daddy, and you always took their side. The truth is I'm not a good enough man to be anyone's father.

July 15, 1943

Looked up and saw five finches on a bush not ten feet from me, three yellow and two red. I'll take that as a sign of something good.

July 15, 1943

I'm working with German prisoners in Flamm's orchards. I know they're supposed to be the enemy, but they look like kids to me, sad and scared and homesick.

What I heard was the United States had more prisoners than they had prisons or places to put them, so they were offered out to farms and orchards as workers. All Mr. Flamm has to do is give them food and lodging, and he gets free workers until the war ends.

They better be glad they're here and not in Russia.

As I follow my trains of thought, a bird sings with all its heart.

July 18, 1943

Did I ever tell you about the time Calamity Jane visited our home town? I heard about it listening to Mormor and her sisters whispering, something about hanging out at the saloon, drinking whiskey, and cussing like a man. I read about it later in the newspaper. The headline was "The Cow Lady of the Black Hills pays Oakes a Short Visit." I wouldn't be surprised if Hildur went to see her.

July 25, 1943

A blow to Hitler; Mussolini quit, stepped down from power. FDR says, "One down and two to go."

August 4, 1943

Mr. Flamm has me out repairing fences on a perfect weather day. Life doesn't get any better.

August 9, 1943

Dug potatoes all morning for Mrs. Flamm.

August 20, 1943

Flamm's peach harvest – we set up tents and picked till 6:00. Then worked in the packing shed 'til about midnight. We packed 75 carloads of peaches. Not sure how I'll feel in the morning, but I bet I sleep well tonight.

September 3, 1943

Allied troops have invaded Salerno.

September 8, 1943

Italy surrendered!

September 16, 1943 My 44th Birthday

I wondered if I should go down to the Army headquarters and try to enlist. I might be too old for the draft, but what if I volunteer?

Then I think, they'll check my records, find out I escaped from a crazy house, and send me back. Maybe I'm a sorry piece of cow dung for not doing my part, but I'm not going back there.

September 21, 1943

Spent most of day picking up a wagon load of windfalls for the cider press. My back is ready for a hot soak and a day off.

September 26, 1943

Dug turnips for Mrs. Flamm

September 30, 1943 Apple Harvest

Today was a big event for the Flamms, with neighbors, workers, and kinfolk gathering for a celebration of the season's end. The women served trays of fried chicken and apple pie while kettles of apple butter cooked over an open fire. The highlight of the event was the barn dance. Good fiddle music is the happiest music I know.

perfect autumn day
summer's last kiss
good-bye

October 28, 1943

Seems like one bad thing follows another, and just when I think things are going great, bam. Life can't get any worse. I'm sitting in a hell hole called Anna City Jail, in the basement of the police station, dark and damp and cold. God, how can people be so hateful? The sheriff picked me up for vagrancy, or so he called it. I was camping for God's sake, taking the weekend off from Flamm's for some fishing and solitude. Seems there's a fine line between camping and vagrancy in this county. Anyway, the asshole's got me, and here I sit.

October 29, 1943

Scream at me to die, go ahead—I deserve it. Why don't you go ahead, kill me, and get it over with.

I'm locked up and can't get out. The devil's got and he's going to kill me. Sweet Jesus, I know I deserve to die. I hate my life. Just let me die.

I heard the police chief talking about transferring me to the State Hospital, said I'm talking to myself and agitated, pacing my cell. I have to stop. I have to calm down. They've locked me up and are going to kill me. Jesus, help me. Jesus, sweet precious holy Jesus, I'm sorry for everything. Help me, if you're real and love me and help me. Don't let them take me there.

Jesus loves me, this I know. For the Bible tells me so. Little ones to Him belong. I'll sing it again and again until I can calm down.

Maybe if I write.

November 1, 1943

Mr. Flamm came by and spoke for me. Said I was a dependable worker and in the end, all the big shot policeman could say was, Yes, sir, but before he let me go, he called me some hateful names I won't write here— said he didn't want to see my face in Anna again. Don't worry. I've had enough. Shaking the dust off my feet, and praying for the good friends like Mr. Flamm, Mr. Lewis, and those families from shanty town I'm leaving behind.

Might be time to check out Nashville.

Mr. Flamm made sure I had what I needed, and Mrs. Flamm packed a pail of food. The Prince Albert can from Boskey Jan I carry in my shirt pocket with my New Testament.

Train goes slow uphill through Cobden; good place to hop a train to the station in Anna for one last good-bye. So long southern Illinois, been nice knowing you.

The Anna to Santa Fe Trail

KARNAK, ILLINOIS

November 12, 1943

When the train slowed south of Karnak, a red-headed woman jumped on and pointed a shot-gun in my direction. She looked at me without talking for a good two minutes, then nodded and introduced herself as Riverboat Bonnie. Said she travels back and forth on the Mississippi between New Orleans and Cairo, mostly on a raft, and the reason was none of my business. As a woman traveling alone, she said she was always on the lookout for an honorable man to partner with, and if I was interested, she'd consider it. Then said, "But don't forget, my shotgun's always loaded."

She went on, "Here's what's in it for you. I'll supply you with food and the most scenic way to travel there is."

I've never been one to pass up an adventure. So I hopped off the train with Bonnie when it slowed at Cairo.

CAIRO, ILLINOIS

November, 14, 1943

Never thought I'd be here, Mark Twain's Promised Land.

Not quite the ideal place Huckleberry thought it was. Bonnie told me the story of one of her uncles who lived here. He was wanted for counterfeiting, but before he got arrested, someone shot him in the face to keep him from talking.

under gray bridge
rowboats carry
nameless men
dressed in darkness
their oars the only sound

November 15, 1943

Bonnie said she had a delivery to make at Fort Defiance.

I went along as far as the gate; then she told me to wait there. I took a walk along the river bank. Splendid scenery.

long-bodied Illinois

dips her toe
at Fort Defiance

Washed dishes for supper at Shemwell's Barbeque.

November 16, 1943

Bonnie spending a lot of time on the barges. Making social connections she says, with her 'don't ask' look. So I'm spending a lot of time in Cairo's public library, reading about town's history.

I need to talk to Bonnie about getting out of here.

I've made friends with the librarian Miss Effie. She gives me history; I give her poems.

Cairo, Illinois

crossroads of a continent
where mobs riot, kill, and burn
and two rivers flow as one

November 17, 1943

Bonnie came running to the raft, all in a dither. Says the Shelton's are in town, whoever they are, and it's time for us to leave, fast.

And finally, we're off!

Floating down the Mississippi is one of the most pleasurable experiences I've ever had. It feels like I *am* the river, flowing past an ever-changing shoreline.

I should write a poem about it.

November 20, 1943

A woman came running out to the edge of the river, waving a handkerchief. Bonnie said, "Keep going, don't even look." I couldn't do it, I had to float close enough to her to call out, ask her what was wrong. About that time, a man came running toward her with a shotgun, and Bonnie yelled, "Dammit, Reuben, get out of here! There's nothing you can do."

Bonnie was right. What could I do? The man shouted, "Keep moving. This is none of your business."

The river's current agreed and quickly carried Bonnie and me downstream, and I was helpless to do a thing. The look in that woman's eyes will stay with me forever.

MEMPHIS, TENNESSEE

December 1, 1943

Talked Miss Bonnie into wintering in Memphis. A river raft in December is not very enjoyable, especially when I'm the one keeping the fire going.

So anyway, we're both out looking for work. Or she's looking and I'm enjoying the sights and sounds of Memphis. My soul dances here.

Nothing like a new town.

December 2, 1943

On a bench across the street from bus station. Weather 's cold, but the sun is shining. I skim the paper for war news, but watching people at the bus station is more interesting.

Then I remember Bonnie and decide I should be looking for work.

December 5, 1943

We're staying in a flop house, better than sleeping outside in December.

Bonnie was out "making connections" and in a cheerful mood tonight. She got out the wine, and we played three games of Michigan Rummy. (She won all three.)

December 6, 1943

Still haven't found work, but at least we have a place to stay, and the soup is free.

December 25, 1943 Christmas Day

Bonnie gave me a bottle of wine for Christmas – I gave her a paperback mystery. We toasted to the New Year and adventures to come.

December 26, 1943

I drank too much wine and now have a God-awful headache, and Bonnie's mad at me for some reason. I'm nothing but a piece of shit.

Tonight she says she's leaving Memphis, and I can come or stay the hell here.

NATCHEZ, MISSISSIPPI

January 3, 1944

We've docked near Natchez, a city high on a bluff overlooking the river. Bonnie said she had some business to attend to.

Spent the afternoon at the library. Read in the newspaper that six million Poles, including three million Jews, have been killed in Nazi death camps.

I have to stop reading about the war.

cold dark cloud covers the sky

Seems like my life is one long hard row to hoe. I don't know what happened to Bonnie; her raft was gone when I came back to camp, no explanation. Good thing I have my satchel and Jan's King Albert can in my pocket. Nothing I need is on that raft.

January 4, 1944

Stormed last night, found a hollow log to crawl into, ugly voices screamed through the night. This morning, I'd die if I could.

Instead, I look to find a jungle, mission, soup kitchen, or even a friendly face. Life goes on.

January 10, 1944

Still no sign of Bonnie. I asked about her at the jungle. Someone said they thought they saw her going into one of the warehouses down by the river—the neighborhood she told me to stay out of.

January 16, 1944 Dorene's Birthday

Dorene, can you ever forgive me?

January 18, 1944 Hildur's Birthday

I miss listening to Hildur playing the piano. She'd play for hours, old church hymns mostly, some classical.

She could sing too – a beautiful contralto. When she was 16, she was part of a quartet that sang in churches—until Father found out it was two boys and two girls, and they were playing cards at practice meetings. That was the end of that.

January 20, 1944

I got hired at the Natchez Country Club, how fine is that? Gardener mostly, but sometimes kitchen and wait staff. Nice bed, steady supply of leftovers, and $10.00 a week. I might stay here awhile.

January 22, 1944

Found the public library. Learned about the well-known slave auction that was north of town. Suddenly this place doesn't feel so friendly.

January 23, 1944

I dreamed I was walking, mile after mile, on a hot dusty road, chained and shackled with a long line of Negroes. A man on horseback rode beside us, whip in one hand, gun in the other. On and on, each time the whip snapped, I felt it. Then I stood with them in a half circle, hat in hand, head down, wearing the same white shirt and corduroy trousers as the others. A woman stood in front of me, began laughing, and pointed in my face, "You're phony and not worth shit!" She pushed me hard, and I fell on the ground, hard enough to wake me up. I checked myself for welts, then held my head and cried.

I don't think I can stay here.

January 26, 1944

As God is my witness, so help me God, I didn't take that man's wallet.

I know when it's time to get out of town.

Too bad, the food was good and the bed clean.

January 27, 1944

Went door to door looking for yard work—got a job cleaning dead brush out of a rich woman's flower bed. Shorter than me by about a foot, she still managed to look down her nose.

I took a break to write a description of this fine day, the puffs of clouds on a baby blue sky, the crisp air and refreshing breeze. She came stomping out and told me to leave, wasn't paying me for vagrancy. I tipped my hat and left with the same empty pockets I came with.

January 29, 1944

how can I write about
   black limbs criss-crossing
   against the sky, when it's
   all I have to say?

shall I describe the cold
   cotton blanket of life
   when my writing is worthless
   to anyone but me?

the sadness of wanting
to be somewhere else, anywhere but here
anyone else but me

January 30, 1944

In the morning. I'll jump a train to New Orleans.

NEW ORLEANS, LOUSIANA

January 31, 1944

You'll never guess who I ran into at the jungle— Riverboat Bonnie. She apologized for having to leave Natchez without me and said,

"Sometimes one needs to get out of town in a hurry." The look on her face reminded me, it's not my business.

I have to say, Bonnie's reasons didn't matter so much, I was enjoying some of the best music I've ever heard. Saxophones, clarinets, accordions, washboards, even spoons, I was glad when they started dancing. People know how to have a good time here.

Bonnie said we were in time for Mardi Gras. I asked what it was, and she said I didn't want to miss it, a celebration of partying and feasting before the fast of Lent, with crowds, parades, and dancing in the streets. I told her I shudder to think about it. She just shook her head.

February 2, 1944

Reading about New Orleans at the library; it's a city divided into two parts, with Canal Street down the center. Modern New Orleans with skyscrapers, wide streets, and electric street cars on one side, and on the other, the old French Quarter with dark and crumbling streets winding through crowded buildings with gabled roofs, red chimneys, and wrought iron balconies. I decided the French Quarter was the side to see.

February 3, 1944

The smell of New Orleans—a combination of boiling shrimp, sweet pastries, river water, and pee.

Have discovered miles and miles of wharves and warehouses. Should be plenty of jobs.

Unfortunately, I was told that the shrimping business is farther south – I guess that hobo in Britt was just blowing wind. But the good news is, the shipyards are hiring workers to build Higgins boats for the war.

I'm not sure what a Higgins boat is, but I'd rather look it up at the library than ask. Too many people think I'm a dumb Swede as it is.

February 5, 1944

At the library again. Learned that a Higgins boat is a flat and shallow ferry, made of plywood, used by service men to land on foreign soil. Can't think of anything I'd rather do – I'd be helping win the war and filling my belly at the same time.

Also read a newspaper article about New Orleans City Park and the six-hundred-year-old oak trees, the famous "Dueling Oaks" where gentlemen settled their disagreements with pistols and children now play. Definitely a place I want to go.

February 6, 1944

Ship yards are not the place for me, all the cussing and smart-mouthing, tough guys wanting to pick a fight. One man asked me if I was a real man or a sissy. Another asked me if my name was Nancy. They all thought that was funny. Then another asked, "You know what we do to queers around here?"

I didn't see much point in defending myself. The money isn't worth it, and the war will get won without me.

February 7, 1944

Found a job washing dishes and cleaning toilets at the Roosevelt Hotel. Two dollars a day plus tips and all the leftovers from the dining room I can eat.

February 8, 1944

Working with an older man who introduced himself as Simon Peter. Told me this was a fine place to work, as long as I didn't mind the ghosts or mafia. He chuckled to himself and walked away.

Later we were alone in the laundry room, and he whispered, "You know this place is run by the mafia, keep your head down and your eyes on what you're doing. They're running a bootleg business in the basement. You'll be bell hopping the crime bosses – you sure you want to do that?"

I told him no, I wasn't sure, but I needed the money. And the food.

"And there's ghosts," he went on. "Children and teachers burned to death on this site back in 1910. I've heard them myself, walking in the hallways, sometimes crying, sometimes laughing. People claim they've seen them."

February 10, 1944

Bob Hope did a show in the Blue Room tonight. I got yelled at for watching instead of clearing tables.

February 14, 1944

Haven't seen Bonnie for a few days. She told me last week she had some business to attend to, then changed the subject.

I've been taking leftovers to Iberville, a public housing project on the edge of French Quarter. Today a young mother came up with a group of kids. She held out her hand and said "Hello, I'm Marguerite." We shook hands, and I noticed she didn't let go right away.

I've never seen anyone like her, wearing orange and purple clothes, colored beads, and dangling earrings. "Come to the parade tonight." she said. "Meet us here."

Well, I went but lasted about 5 minutes, then got away as fast as I could. I'm now sitting at City Park, alone under a wide oak tree, my back against its bark, listening to a songbird and breathing deeply the quiet air.

Mardi Gras, what's that behind your mask?

February 15, 1944

I dosed off in the hotel's warm laundry room and had a terrible dream. Must have thought too much about Simon's story and then that parade and noisy crowd. I heard children laughing, the laughing turned to screaming, and the screaming got louder and louder until I woke up.

And then, I swear, I saw a young girl in the hallway. She asked me where her daddy was, then vanished into thin air. Oh God, Dorene. What have I done?

February 16, 1944

Got to shine Louis Armstrong's shoes today. He smiled from ear to ear, thanked me, and gave me a 25-cent tip. He told me he's singing tonight in the Blue Room, and I should come see.

Back in Iberville again this afternoon. The hotel throws away more food than the help can eat.

Marguerite came with a paper bag she said was a gift for me. Back in my hotel room I see there are a half dozen square doughnuts, covered with powdered sugar, and light as a feather. I've eaten three.

February 17, 1944

Last night Mr. Armstrong played the trumpet like I've never heard before. I couldn't help but be happy when I heard him sing "What a Wonderful World." It is a wonderful world, Dorene. No matter what, I hope you know that too.

February 20, 1944

I saw a woman shot and killed tonight. It was during a busy time, a crowd of people coming and going but no one seemed to see but me. I turned the other way pretty fast so maybe the shooter didn't see me. Dammit, it's what I get for not keeping my head down.

Simon told me later she was the girlfriend of a snitch, and it was payback killing. Maybe this isn't such a great place to work after all.

February 28, 1944

Marguerite sent a note telling me to come to her house right away. She had something important to tell me. Of course, I went. She said, "Reuben, you've got to get away from the Roosevelt! I've heard from one of Carlos Marcello's drivers, they know you saw the shooting. The killer wasn't alone. You're on their hit list!"

Oh God, now what. I don't know who Marcello is, but I can guess. I know how to get out of town in a hurry, but Marguerite went on, "It's not safe for you even to go back and get your things. Stay here in Iberville; we'll hide you until things settle down."

That seems like the best choice, just disappear for a while. I'm good at that too.

March 1, 1944

I'm staying in a shed behind Marguerite's, not showing my face. When it's dark, she brings me food, water, and news if there's any.

March 3, 1944

Marguerite came with my bedroll and satchel, smiled, and said she had connections.

March 10, 1944

Marguerite came and told me the coast was clear. The shooter has been shot.

That doesn't mean I'm going back to work at the Roosevelt. Marguerite said I was welcome to the shed, and I could work for food. Sounds good, but first I'm going to try to find Bonnie and let her know where I am.

March 11, 1944

Left word in the jungle for Bonnie, to come to Iberville and ask for Marguerite.

March 14, 1944

Bonnie came to visit, said she was glad to hear from me. She's staying with friends in a stilt camp on Lake Pontchartrain. I asked if she knew of any work. She didn't but said she'd keep her ears open.

"Let me know if you leave town," she said when she left. Then she whispered, "Be careful of that woman. I know what I'm talking about."

March 25, 1944

Reading the paper, mass killing near Rome, German soldiers slaughtered almost 400 Jews and Italian prisoners. Oh God, I don't want to think about it— I can't *stop* thinking about it.

April 9, 1944 Easter Sunday

I'm spending Easter at City Park with Marguerite and her kids. Big parade and Easter egg hunt. I can almost pretend I have a family.

May 14, 1944 Mother's Day

colored feathers, left on park bench
the smell of your perfume
do I hear you whisper?

June 5, 1944

I'm staying with Marguerite for the time being, helping her around the house, fixing things and babysitting in exchange for room and board. She treats me nice, and her food is good too.

June 18, 1944 Father's Day

Father had a rich bass voice; I wish you could have heard him in the choir.

He didn't understand my poetry, called it shirking my work. I can still hear his booming voice yelling at me to get off my butt and get to work.

I disappointed him, he didn't try to hide it. He claimed if it was up to me, I'd be a shiftless bum. He wasn't too far wrong, was he?

July 4, 1944

Went to St. Louis Cemetery. I read about it and wanted to see for myself, all above-ground, people buried in stone rooms. Interesting to read the headstones – politicians, pirates, heroes of the Battle of New Orleans.

I was enjoying my day, thinking I'd sit in the sunshine somewhere and write a description of this place, when I came to the tomb of Voodoo Queen Maria Leveau. It was decorated with beads, candles, bones, and even cigarettes, and a sign for how to contact her. A cold breeze came suddenly from nowhere, and I decided I better leave.

And then I heard her. Laughing, mocking me when I started running. I felt something heavy hit me in the back, and I fell forward. A weight covered me, and I couldn't move, couldn't breathe. Then about the time I thought it was over and I was going to die, the weight was gone, just like that. I got up and came back to the jungle.

Have been reading poetry.

August 1, 1944

Marguerite was giving me a haircut when a man pushed open the door and yelled, "What the hell is going on here?" He shoved Marguerite against the wall, then turned to me with an open switchblade.

Kids crying, Marguerite screaming, "Stop, you're making a mistake!" He poked the end of his knife under my chin and said, "If I see you around my wife again, I'll cut your heart out."

I'll try to get word to Bonnie. I'm leaving tonight, hitchhiking to anywhere but here.

TUSCALOOSA, ALABAMA

August 2, 1944

cold morning
I push my face
against the wind

What can I do but keep moving? I got a ride with a college student heading back to school at the University of Alabama in Tuscaloosa. When he asked where I was going, I asked, "Where you headed?" So here I am in Tuscaloosa (ancestral home of the Chief Tuskaloosa or Black Warrior, a Muskogean—my ride was full of information.) Found a soup line for lunch. I'll look for work tomorrow.

Camping by Black Warrior River, I watch ripples flowing downstream, dancing with the shoreline.

August 15, 1944

First Father and then you, I couldn't do anything right. Dammit, Laura.

Doctors said I was *insane*. What does that mean? Darn doctors don't know everything.

I just watched men wearing white hoods, carrying burning torches, push a black man into the woods. And they call *me* insane?

August 17, 1944

Meet the new grounds keeper for Indian Hills Country Club. I mow grass, trim hedges, pull weeds, and collect golf balls—$2.00 a day and a bed in the basement, good enough for me.

August 28, 1944

Paris is liberated – the Germans have surrendered. General de Gaulle has returned, shouting "Viva Paris!"

November 7, 1944

President Roosevelt elected for a 4th term, first time in the history of the US that we've had a president this popular.

November 11, 1944 Martin's Goose Day

Marten Gas Day for Swedes. Every year on November 11, we'd have a feast of roast goose to celebrate the end of fall planting. Women cooked bread stuffings with apples, prunes, sauerkraut and green cabbage, and made what they call 'blood soup', seasoning the blood, heart, liver, neck and wings of the goose with apples, prunes, ginger, vinegar and sugar. I can almost taste it now.

November 23, 1944 Thanksgiving Day.

Eating pumpkin pie down by the river. One of the waiters said it was left over from the country club's big dinner. He gave it to me instead of throwing it out.

So here I am on Thanksgiving Day, alone and eating what rich people throw away. I should die and get it over with.

November 26, 1944

Trouble finds me wherever I am. Some big shot with too much brandy accused me taking cash from his locker. As God is my witness, I didn't do it. Unfortunately, Mr. Big Shot is a big spender and I'm nobody, so I left in a hurry. Good thing I don't have much to pack.

December 25, 1944 Christmas Day

I have nothing to write. I hate my life, I'm a piece of shit, and there's nothing else to say.

January 16, 1945 Dorene's Birthday

You're twelve today. Have probably had your first Communion and been confirmed. And I missed it.

January 18. 1945 Hildur's Birthday

After Hildur graduated from 8th grade in the one-room school house in Hample. Father had a hard time deciding about sending her to high school. It meant she'd have to be boarded in Oakes, and he was so protective and worried about everything – then a minister with kids in high school offered to have her stay with them. Father felt secure about this kind of family so he agreed. He would have had conniptions and brought her home immediately if he knew what went on there – those kids had a reputation for being wild and crazy—I think Hildur was having the time of her life.

I would like to see you again, Hildur. I think of you often, wishing I could let you know I'm alive, that some days life is good. Then I remember how worthless I am, and I'm ashamed to be your brother. You're better off without me.

January 28, 1945

"GERMAN ARMY DEFEATED—Ending the Battle of the Bulge." Newspaper says it was the largest and bloodiest battle yet, with around 200,000 casualties. I can't imagine it. I can't think about it. Will this war never end?

April 12, 1945

A sad day for America, President Roosevelt had a stroke and died. Probably too much stress and pressure—I think four terms as president would kill anyone.

Harry Truman is our new president.

April 25, 1945

I'm at Bryce Hospital for the Insane, Father Carmichael from the mission called them to come get me. I didn't know it until they showed up to take me away. Dammit, he could have warned me. I can pull myself together. I don't need to be here.

Sitting here outside the admissions office with my journal, trying to calm down. I know they're going to kill me.

This place is too quiet. All I hear is my foot tapping, echoing down a long hallway. I'm writing to calm myself. The walls are the same color green as in the Insane Asylum in Iowa, even the pattern in the floor tile is the same. The air is thick with disinfectant. I'm sick to my stomach.

God help me.

LINCOLN, ILLINOIS

April 27, 1945

Here I am, back in Lincoln. Got away from Bryce as fast as I could. Sitting in that hallway, I watched two men pushing and shoving a screaming crying man in a straightjacket, and something inside me snapped. I got up, discovered the door to the lobby was open, and I was free to go. Go I did. Ran as fast as I could.

Ran through the hospital's cemetery—rows of numbered, nameless tombstones. I ran even faster.

Jumped a train, then hitchhiked, and have made my way to Cherry's. She's better for my disposition than any mental hospital.

Cherry fixed a meal to remember with some of her special tea to calm my nerves. She insisted on washing my clothes and bed roll – couldn't remember the last time they were clean.

April 28, 1945

Cherry's invited me to stay awhile, no strings attached.

April 30, 1945

During supper Cherry got on the subject of politics, how wonderful a man named Earl Browder was. Said his explanation of communism and socialism made sense, and the reforms he wanted would solve America's problems. She called herself a "liberal internationalist" whatever that means. I had no idea what she was talking about, but the food was delicious. Fried chicken, mashed potatoes, and of course, cherry pie.

May 1, 1945

Cherry turned on the radio first thing this morning to hear the news: Hitler and his wife have killed themselves. "The world is such a wicked place," Cherry said. I thought she was going to cry.

May 8, 1945

GERMANY HAS SURRENDERED!

A heavy cloud has been lifted. I take a deep breath—seems like a long time since I could.

May 21, 1945 Laura's Birthday

Laura, I loved your laugh. How I'd love to hear it now.

May 23, 1945

Cherry can't seem to talk about anything but politics, Earl Browder and now Karl Marx. Good time of year to follow the geese again.

Picked a bouquet of black-eyed Susans and left them in a mason jar on Cherry's porch.

BELLE PLAINE, IOWA

July 31, 1945

Hopped off the train at Belle Plaine, just for the chance I might get a glimpse of you – hung around town, keeping out of sight. Luck was with me, and I saw you and your mom going into A & P.

You look beautiful, by the way. Tall and willowy like Mother. You have my eyes.

Went to a hobo camp outside of Luzerne and did some asking around. I met Bo who introduced himself as the town drunk. He told me what happened after I went to the Insane Asylum. Laura was declared destitute by the state, her older boys were taken from her and put in an orphanage in Davenport, Laura and Dorene moved in with her parents, and I have a new son.

This page is stained with teardrops.

BRITT, IOWA

August 3, 1945

Back at Britt. Usually I'd rather stay to myself, but when I'm here, with like-minded friends around a bonfire, I'm a different man. I can sit here for hours, visiting and sharing music, poetry, storytelling—and no one knows my name or cares.

Later Connecticut Red asked me to write out my poem, "The Legend of Davy Getz." It's from a true story I heard in a jungle somewhere.

Dayton remembers
the death of Davy Getz
thirty-nine years old
mind of a child

captured in a war
he didn't understand
carrying an open rifle
hunting squirrels he said

tied to a wagon
a rope around his neck
he staggered behind
their procession through the Valley

on a grassy knoll
forced to dig his own grave
elderly parents begging

bystanders pleading
he was shot

General Custer's orders
no exceptions
this is war

you'll die a bloody death for this!
an onlooker yelled

not everyone knows
about the death of Davy Getz
most everyone's heard
of Custer's

Virginia Slim said I should make into a ballad, said he'd sing it. I told him I'd try, but I'm not much good rhyming or counting syllables.

August 4, 1945

Quiet in the camp this morning. I like being the first awake, getting the fire started for coffee and breakfast, having time to sit and write in my journal, alone with you, Dorene. I pretend I'm talking to you, that you're here with me. This morning, I'll tell you some good memories.

Father, Hildur, and I went to Oakes on Saturday nights to sell our eggs and cream. It was the high point of our week. All the farmers came to town, the stores stayed open, and people visited up and down the street. Father would treat us to a hamburger and milk shake.

Another special memory, Father made root beer in the basement. He believed a hard day's work in the heat required some refreshment. Add a scoop of homemade ice cream and we had a summer treat.

If I could spend one day with you, Dorene, I think we'd go somewhere for a root beer float.

Nice while it lasted. Folks are waking up.

August 5, 1945

Made a new friend this morning, goes by Montana Man or Tan Man for short. He laughs and his eyes laugh with him. A young man, maybe in his late 20's, he used to be an English teacher but the school calendar was too confining. He chuckled and said he's been accused of being a hobo. It started one summer vacation when he and a friend decided to hitchhike and backpack up and down the state of California. Now he calls himself a traveling poet and has traveled back and forth across the United States, sharing poetry in boxcars and jungles.

He said beauty is everywhere, but he likes Montana the best. He's planning to go back for the Black Foot Powwow, told me he has business to take care of, then changed the subject to talk about how big and blue the Oklahoma sky is, and did I want to travel with him?

So now I'm riding on a flatcar beside Tan, just sitting here enjoying the scenery and the sky, and my, what sky it is.

PAWHUSKA, OKLAHOMA

August 7, 1945

colors of Oklahoma—
cinnamon, paprika
straw tan, bronze gold
and bright, bright, blue

Tan and I jumped off when the train slowed for Pawhuska. We've made ourselves a camp beside a small pond, surrounded by dried grasses and dwarfed oak trees. He suggested we fish for our supper.

We made a good catch, and while the fish was cooking on sticks over a fire, Tan talked about his favorite poems and quoted Robert Frost, "Poetry is a way of taking life by the throat." We were both quiet for a while, then Tan said, "Swede, it's almost time." He got up and walked away.

August 8, 1945

Left camp before Tan woke up. Took a walk north of Pawhuska through some of the most glorious landscape I've ever seen—tall prairie grasses mixed with hundreds of wildflowers, birds flitting here and there, as far as the eye can see—never seen anything like it. Wonder what Father would say, if he could see me now.

Probably something about not working.

A strong wind came later in the afternoon, blowing almost horizontally. I saw a butterfly down in some grasses, beating its wings against the wind but unable to fly. I picked it up, made a cup for it with my hands, and brought it with me.

I made the butterfly a nest in a can, put in some flowers. The next day, it was crawling around the camp, even on my arm. Tan was most impressed.

Lesson of the Butterfly

oh butterfly with
broken wing
beaten by prairie winds
will you dance in
my cup of flowers
drink sweet nectar
beside my bed?

will you teach me
how to live
while you teach me
how to die?

Saw my first buffalo, heavy-headed and sad.

August 9, 1945

Tan and I decided we better find some work. Went to the jungle in Pawhuska and heard that the Comstock and Drummond ranches were hiring help with branding. We walked out to the highway and put our thumbs out, and it just so happened, the first person who stopped was in a pickup heading toward the Drummonds. We jumped in the back.

I told Mr. Drummond I'd never branded before but was willing to learn. He laughed and said, "Not much to it, you just catch 'em, hold 'em down, and lay the hot iron on 'em!"

After the first calf, its screams cutting through my heart, I said, "This job is not for me," and walked away. Tan told me wait, he was coming with me.

Back at the jungle for mulligan, still hearing that calf. The look on Tan's face says he hears it too.

August 10, 1945

Two cardinals in camp this morning.

Tan and I went to Pawhuska Library to check war headlines. We found out that on Monday, the United States dropped an atomic bomb on Hiroshima, killing about 140,000 people. It doesn't seem real and maybe that's better. I won't think about it.

Then I read about Chief Standing Bear and his lesson of forgiveness. "My hand is not the color of yours, but if I pierce it, I shall feel pain. If you pierce your hand, you also feel pain. The blood that will flow from mine will be the same color as yours. I am a man. The same God made us both."

August 11, 1945

at Lake Pawhuska
one last lingering look

good-bye to grasses
whose names I don't know

to dwarfed pines on chiseled hills
rocky red soil and calico pastures

to an open sky of ultimate blue

I like to pretend I understand birdsong; the chirps and warbles are words, and they're saying life is good, the world is beautiful, be happy.

Tonight, after our feast of fish over the campfire, Tan told me about the 'hot iron in his heart.' He said he was married to a Black Foot woman named Nancy Yellow Feather. He told me how beautiful she was and how much they loved each other.

Then he stood up and looked at me with tears in his eyes, He almost whispered that one morning he woke to find she'd been stabbed to death right next to him in bed. And he knew who did it.

"He's going to pay. I've let him think he's safe awhile, but when he least suspects it, he's going to pay. When that sonofabitch breathes his last breath. I want him looking at my face."

August 12, 1945

Spent the night in an abandoned farm house. I swear I heard real voices, a woman crying, a man calling her name. Then the woman left, and the man's voice got louder and louder until it woke me up. They didn't seem to notice I was there, but I still felt like I was trespassing and left first thing this morning.

forty-five miles
west of Ponca City
pioneer cemetery
Mulligans, Rickets, Buffalous

two lone trees

perfect place of rest for my friend the butterfly, who lived with me for two weeks and died peacefully

Tan's heading back to the reservation, says he sleeps better with a drumbeat. He slapped me on the shoulder, and said, "Hang in there, Swede. Hope to see you again." He gave me this poem,

Harvest Train

stepped from tracks up on train
Jackson line, Jonesboro Station
wayfarer, roundtrip, first leg
stranger on a sentimental journey

GM & O Rebel, traveling
through landscapes of the soul
to stations of the mind
restoring beauty along the way

stepped from train down on tracks
Jackson Line, Jonesboro Station
dream-keeper, round trip, last leg
pilgrim from a sacred journey home

August 13, 1945

Went out to Comstock's to ask about a couple hours work, just not branding. Mr. Comstock said, "Sure, I've got a field full of boulders. See how many you can clear out."

Of course, I had to do it like a Swede, and stacked the rocks in neat circles along the fence rows. When I got back up to the house, Mrs. Comstock invited me to sit on the porch. One of the girls brought me some cold tea and a dinner of pinto beans and brisket, fried okra, and the best chocolate cake I've ever had. When I thanked her for it, she told me it was the Comstock family-favorite Wesson Oil Cake and did I want another piece? Of course, I said yes, please. She offered to copy the recipe if I wanted. Here it is, for you, Dorene.

Mrs. Comstock's Wesson Oil Cake

3 cups flour
2 cups sugar
3 teaspoons baking soda
½ cup cocoa
1 teaspoon salt
2 eggs
1 cup Wesson oil
1 cup buttermilk
1 teaspoons vanilla
1 cup boiling water

Mix together all the dry ingredients. Add eggs, oil, buttermilk, and vanilla. Mix well. Add the boiling water and mix well. Pour into 2 9-inch cake pans, well-greased and floured. Bake 30-45 minutes at 350°.

So, with two dollars in my pocket and a piece of cake for the road, I'm hitchhiking on Route 66, southwest across Oklahoma, on my way to Santa Fe.

August 14, 1945 Victory Day

I heard it on the radio, a world away from this wide-open Oklahoma sky. The war is over. We won. Our troops are coming home. Everyone is cheering and celebrating and I'm here, alone with this stranger giving me a ride. He doesn't talk, just stares straight ahead. Maybe he didn't hear?

I see his hands squeeze the steering wheel and pretend I don't notice. Glad to hop out of his truck at the next stop.

CHEROKEE, OKLAHOMA

August 19, 1945

Walked to a town called Cherokee and saw a sign for a Mennonite Church. I remembered the kindness (and good cooking) of the Mennonites in Sterling and headed their way.

An older man by the name of Ben Wenger said he could use me a couple days with harvest, if I was interested. Of course, I said yes.

August 20, 1945

Staying in Wenger's barn, writing by kerosene lamp, listening to mourning doves. They sound so sad and resigned, singing, coo-coo-coo, this is the way it is, again and again.

I bet we harvested 100 bushels of corn by hand today, tossing the corn into a horse-drawn box wagon, then scooping it into a crib. We worked until the evening meal.

I was invited to eat with them, men and boys on one side of a long table, women and girls on the other. Mr. Wenger cleared his throat, and everyone bowed their head for silent prayer. When Mr. Wenger reached for a dish to pass, everyone did the same. A simple feast of boiled sweet corn, fried chicken, gravy, and biscuits. After the meal, Mr. Wenger stood up and announced it was time for bed.

August 22, 1945

I happened to visit their church on a day when there was a picnic afterward. I enjoyed watching the children play. Laughing, running, rosy-cheeked innocence. Boys in straw hats; girls braided and barefoot.

August 25, 1945

Sitting out on a porch swing, a bird sings pretty-pretty-pretty

Two children, a girl about seven and her younger brother, came and sat beside me. Didn't say anything at first, just smiled and looked away. I started the conversation, asking about school and guessing their ages. They were soon both talking at once, telling me a story about their horse that fell down on purpose, in the middle of a busy road. Their mother tried to get him to stand up but wasn't having any success. Finally, their cousin came to the rescue. Mary said John started crying; John said he did not, Mary did.

Mrs. Wenger showed me a book of Mennonite history and folk sayings. I liked these: "It's no use boiling your cabbage twice," "The wise man has long ears and a short tongue," and "A willing worker doesn't wait till he's asked." Good words to live by.

August 28, 1945

There's been an accident. A young neighbor with family fell from the top of the grain elevator in Ingersoll, broke every bone in his body. Another widow, another fatherless child.

Sunday singing, they sound like angels in heaven. No organ, just their voices in perfect harmony.

Corncribs are full; I'm heading out in the morning.

GUYMON, OKLAHOMA

August 30, 1945

Passing through Guymon, I stopped by rodeo grounds and asked for work in exchange for food. The cowboy I talked too didn't look friendly, but he asked if I'd clean the holding pens. I told him yes, sir. He handed me a shovel and pail and pointed to me where to go.

Stench so strong, brought tears to my eyes, but I worked two hours straight, scooping manure and dumping bucket after bucket of the stuff into a pile behind the arena. (I figured out why cowboys wear bandanas over their noses.)

When I finished, Mr. Cowboy handed me a dollar bill and a bucket full of fried chicken, cold potatoes, and biscuits. Then he tipped his hat and wished me well.

Spending the night under the open sky, just west of Jet, beside a great salt lake. I watch Osage women collect salt, brushing it up with turkey feathers, and then scraping it into baskets that they carry on their heads.

BOISE CITY, OKLAHOMA

August 31, 1945

In the back of a model-T pick-up, I try to paint the scenery with words:

> red earth wears a carpet of sage green
> ragged ravines snake out of sight
> lonely windmills of weathered wood
> whisper to a bright blue sky

Church bells play "I sing the Almighty Power of God". I used to sing that song with all my heart, in Swedish. I tried to sing it now, but I've forgotten the words.

September 2, 1945

My shoes have worn through the bottom, my feet are blistered. I went through trash to find cardboard to cut new soles. Things will be better in Santa Fe.

September 4, 1945

Longest road I've ever walked; finally have a ride.

September 5, 1945

I'm amazed by this landscape—never-ending horizon in every direction. I've seen pictures, but they're nothing like this.

September 7, 1945

Life, what's it for without a legacy? One hundred years from now, will anyone know or care that I lived?

I don't mind working when I have to. When I have a job, I do my best. I just don't believe in working when I *don't* have to – there are things more important, like watching the world go by and writing in my journal.

CLAYTON, NEW MEXICO

September 8, 1945

I walk into a new town, stand up straight, and pretend I'm somebody.

Got a job first place I went – a hotel ran by Swedes. I offered to clean spittoons or do anything that needed done—maybe they could see the Swede in me, but right away the owner said, sure, we can use you. So I'm now an official employee of the grand Eklund Hotel in Clayton, New Mexico. I have a room in the basement and all I can eat. Life doesn't get much better.

I asked about the bullet holes in the saloon ceiling. Mrs. Eklund told me that in 1905 some of Harding's supporters, celebrating his election, fired their pistols into the ceiling. She didn't think anyone was hurt. I was hoping for a story a little more exciting.

Mrs. Eklund sure does get me distracted from my work. She's found eager ears for stories about the history of this wild-west town, so different from where I grew up in Oakes, North Dakota.

Black Jack Ketchum is her favorite story, telling the tale of his lawless years and the details of his hanging. She showed me pictures of the eventful day, when for some reason, his head severed from his body. "Ironic, isn't it," she said, "Black Jack spent his life as a notorious bank robber, to be remembered for something as humiliating as a botched hanging." Oh well, Mr. Eklund doesn't seem to mind my relaxed schedule, with so much time for conversation. I think he appreciates his wife having someone to talk to. (Mr. Eklund doesn't talk much.)

September 9, 1945

Leisurely morning in my room. Only one guest last night, and I've got the place pretty well clean.

Went to lobby and saw headline: JAPAN HAS SURRENDERED! THE WAR IS OVER! They found out what happens when you start a fight with the US – two atomic bombs later, what could they do but give up?

September 10, 1945

I've been accused of taking a woman's jewelry. Mrs. Eklund is standing up for me, but threats of police involvement are causing me to shorten my time in Clayton. As soon as Mr. Eklund gets back with my pay, I'm heading out.

Following the Santa Fe Trail, countless others drawn by the same mysterious force that's drawing me. I want to see 'this city different in the land of enchantment" I've heard so much about.

GLADSTONE, NEW MEXICO

September 11, 1945

Got dropped off at the Gladstone Mercantile. My ride has a ranch just north of here and said this was as far as he was going. Fine with me. I want to do some exploring anyway. The sky is amazing, looks like a big blue bowl overturned on top of us.

I stare across the horizon, where sky meets earth, countless miles away, a blurred line of sage and blue.
And I breathe.

Went into the mercantile, looked around awhile, then sat down at the only table. A woman introduced herself as Thelma and asked if I'd like something to eat. I told her I was a traveling field worker and asked if she had anything I could do for a meal. She said she had some left-over elk stew I could have for nothing. Free coffee, too.

Thelma asked if I'd ever seen a place so sparse. I told her I never imagined it.

I had to ask, what was it like, living here, miles from everywhere, a tiny speck beneath a limitless sky. She laughed and said, "We're used to it I guess. We love it here and wouldn't want to live anywhere else."

I decided to stick around a week or two and asked if she knew of any work. She said the bean farms in Farley might be hiring.

The woman in the post office gave me directions. Before I went, I walked a way out from the store, explored an old school house and an old stone foundation, found a bleached cow skull, an agate marble, and some rusted farm tools.

Sat down and wrote this poem:

Gladstone

welcome oasis under
high desert sun
population sparse as landscape
windswept and prairie strong

between Clayton and Springer
ninety-mile expanse with
no other tonic
for this tired traveler's soul

at mile marker thirty-six
I stop to stretch
communicate with humanity
ask, what's life like

under this massive sapphire sky and
three hundred sixty degrees of horizon

beneath such infinite blue
does your scope match your sphere,
your honesty match this firmament?
can there be any secrets,
can a speck hide from
a God the size of heaven?

welcome, smiles Thelma
owner of Gladstone Mercantile
artist of cowboy cooking and southwest décor,
stop awhile and linger
experience roots deep in treasured past

stroll around the ruins
explore the flotsam and jetsam
of prairie winds and desert sun
examine primordial remnants
of long ago ranches
a wagon-rutted trail

feel the same dry sun and scratching wind
felt centuries before

you see,
hardship makes us strong and
openness sets us free

thank you, Gladstone
I tip my hat

Thelma says people live a long time in Gladstone.

FARLEY, NEW MEXICO

September 12, 1945

Farley depot, whistle stop on Santa Fe Trail. Looks like about five or six families live here. Walked around town, surprised to see a big public school. Kids must come from a hundred miles around.

Found a job with the first person I talked to, a man named Dub Brown. He offered me a dollar a day with a cot in a bean crib. Good enough.

September 13, 1945

Started work this morning with a crew of young local boys, using a pitch fork to pile rows of already cut beans. The boys so happy and cheerful under the bright New Mexican sun, I couldn't help but enjoy myself.

One of them was John Perkins, as tall and long as I am, polite, well-mannered, and quiet. The boy named Wayne, on the other hand, was a rowdy smart-aleck, but he had us all laughing. He claimed he could ride a bull and lasso a wild pony at the same time, then pretended he was doing it. John reminded him we were getting paid for working. Wayne called him a name I won't repeat, but then he grinned and nobody got mad.

They talked about the dances on Saturday nights. John said a man named Bob Wills, the king of swing, was coming to the next one, with his Texas Cowboys. He said I should be sure to come if I like good music. I just might.

September 16, 1945

You won't believe who I saw at the dance last night, Jan Curry, one of the girls who visited my campsite in Boskeydell, Illinois, or Boskey Jan as she reminded me, traveling with the band, dressed like a cowgirl and wearing a guitar.

I asked about her parents, she shrugged and looked away – said she hadn't seen them in a while. "They don't understand. I want to make music and dance, see the world, have some fun. Everyone expects me to do this and that. I got so bored, I just wanted to die. I had to get away."

I gave her all the reasons I could think of for why she should go home. I could tell she wasn't listening.

Wayne didn't take long to set his cap for Jan and start showing off. He'd had too much to drink, was throwing beer bottles in the air and shooting at them with a pistol. Jan cheered and clapped and that just egged him on. Then he said, "Let's leave this party, see what's going on in Raton." Jan didn't hesitate - she and three other young people jumped into his car. He squealed his tires as he left.

Sad to say, there was a car accident, Wayne driving too fast, rolled the car going around a curve. Wayne was killed, another of the boys with a broken back. Jan left without saying good-bye.

September 16, 1945 My 46th Birthday

Sunday morning walks, the best part of the week. Today I explored north of town, went about five miles and found a church and cemetery, so beautiful and well-cared for—with nothing but horizon in every direction. I spent some time walking around the tombstones, looking through the church window and wondering, who on earth does this? And why?

I got the feeling I was being watched and left without looking back.

September 20, 1945

We were all working out in the field, Mr. Brown with us, using pitchforks to make piles of cut bean stalks. A thunderstorm came up—we ran for cover in the trucks parked at the end of the field, carrying our pitchforks over our shoulders. A lightning bolt struck Mr. Brown's—he died instantly.

Two deaths in a week. Time for me to move on.

September 23, 1945

lone dove
song of solitude
on gray wire

I don't know how much more I can take. Miles and miles of endless road, not a tree in sight. I'm out of food and water. Is this the way I'm going to die?

Thank God, I finally got a ride. An old Mexican in a rusted pick-up, offered not only a ride all the way to Santa Fe but a drink of cold water, too. He said his name was Francesco, smiled big, and shook my hand.

He could tell I wasn't from around here, so he pointed out the landmarks, Rabbit Ears, my first mountains, and Wagon Mound, a mountain that really looks like a covered wagon. He said we were traveling the old Cimarron Trail, a dangerous by-pass on the original Santa Fe Trail. He told about bandits and outlaws and people disappearing. I was glad when he changed the subject and offered me some of his wife's tamales.

SANTA FE, NEW MEXICO

October 1, 1945

Francesco brought me all the way to the Plaza, said this was the end of the trail, the heart of Santa Fe. I shook his hand and thanked him again. He put his hand over mine and said, "Adios, mi amigo. Go with God, my friend."

I watch people
and the gray wave
of doves as they land

I close my eyes
feel the sun on my face
breathe deep the piñon air

sunshine smells like
roasting chilés

Asked another hobo on the Plaza for advice on getting a job. He said, "Go to Mission Viejo and get a shower, throw those overalls in the trash, put on a clean shirt and better shoes, then go to La Fonda Hotel. They're always looking for bell hops and housekeepers."

He gave me directions to the mission. I've had a bath; this bed feels wonderful. I'll check out La Fonda in the morning.

October 3, 1945

Happy to say, I have a job, with afternoons off for 'siesta'. First thing I did after changing beds and cleaning toilets for two hours was find the public library. Spent the whole afternoon looking at pictures of the trees, wildflowers, and birds of New Mexico, enjoying their names, and the new world opening before me.

New Mexico—It's life in bright light, crisp air, and cool breeze. A poet's paradise.

October 5, 1945

with gold brush
afternoon sun
paints the desert

October 7, 1945

How many ways are there to say, "God, I'm glad to be here?"

Mountain views, adobe buildings, and the biggest blue sky I've ever seen.

New Mexico sunrise
flows down the mountains
paints awake the desert

Beauty beyond what I ever imagined.

Spent time with some artists on Canyon Road. They create poetry with paint.

If heaven was a color, it'd be turquoise.

October 11, 1945

Back at the library. A city with 400 years of history is bound to have some stories to tell.

I read that early Indians called the location of Santa Fe "Dancing Ground of the Sun." I can see why – sunlight does dance here, with colors, lines, and shadows and an everchanging view

October 26, 1945

A big reunion this week at La Fonda, former governors and big shots, descendants of the original signers of the state's constitution, smoking fat cigars and looking important, I might as well be invisible. I can tell you, their shit smells as bad as any. Working through our 'siesta' time, just to keep up.

They've got me helping in the restaurant, La Plazuela. I'm enjoying the music, a mariachi band—four Mexican cowboys with an accordion, cello, and two guitars, playing polkas and waltzes, wearing embroidered jackets, tight black pants, and wide-brimmed hats. After every song, they shout, "Ayyyajajaaaaiii!" and "Viva Méjico!" I know this much, I'd rather be dancing, than cleaning tables.

By midnight, I was having a hard time paying attention to my job and accidently dropped a tray of dishes, breaking glass everywhere. Everyone stopped and looked, then my boss came out yelling and said he was docking my pay to buy new dishes. God, I can't do anything right.

October 27, 1945

One of the big shots, I won't say his name, came up and handed me a five-dollar bill, said there was more if I wanted it. He was looking for someone to run errands for him to Tres Penos, Mexico. Something about his voice gave me the chills. I gave him the money back and started to walk the other way. He put his hand on my shoulder and said, "You're not too smart, are you? I'm offering you easy money." The only thing I could think of was to keep walking. I could hear a stream of cuss words following me, but I didn't care.

November 1, 1945

A man named Sam Martinez introduced himself in the laundry room, said I looked like a good man but a green horn. He wanted to warn me about a smuggling business, said to stay away from any deal that seemed too good to be true. I laughed and said, "Too late, it's already happened. Don't worry, I'm not as dumb as I look."

He shook his head and said, "Keep your eyes open, Swede."

November 22, 1945 Thanksgiving Day

Thanksgiving with the Martinez family at Cochiti Pueblo. First time I've had tamales with turkey, but it was a delicious meal, with corn pudding, green chili, cinnamon tortillas, and pumpkin flan.

December 25, 1945 Christmas Day

Christmas in Santa Fe is something to see. The city glows with lights and bon-fires, piñon and cedar smoke fills the air, and crowds of carolers walk the winding streets, singing with all their hearts. I can see my breath it's so cold, but I'm walking and singing like everyone else, pretending I belong here.

December 30, 1945

Headline of today's Albuquerque Journal: Two Nazi Generals Hanged by Russians. I couldn't read it. I can't even think about it—it's like one cold hand squeezes my heart and another is around my throat.

January 16, 1946 Dorene's 13th Birthday

Someday I'd like to go to Skőne, Sweden and take you with me, Dorene. We'd find the old Martinson homestead, the family dance pavilion, maybe walk the cemeteries where my grandparents and all the grandparents before them are buried. We'd hold hands, explore our history together.

We could pretend we're a happy family, and I'm not a worthless man who couldn't be a father. I wish I was dead.

January 18, 1946 Hildur's Birthday

Hildur's boyfriend was Ernest – one of the boys in the church quartet she was part of. They were good, too—traveled around to different churches for special services. Father forbid her from seeing him after he found out they were playing cards. He wasn't happy that Ernest had a car either, called him a flashy show-off who wouldn't amount to anything.

I knew Hildur was seeing him anyway, but I didn't tell. They ended up running away together. She sent me a letter from California, letting me know they were married. I haven't seen her since.

January 30, 1946

Tan found me at La Fonda, said I wasn't hard to find. Good to have friends in the jungle. Glad to see him again; we made plans to meet on the Plaza when I got off work.

He says he's sleeping under the stars up in the national forest, washing dishes at Plaza Diner for food, what more could a man want?

He asked about me. I had to admit, I'm doing pretty well here, too. I try not to think too much, just enjoy the sunshine and beauty around me.

I told him I'd made some friends from Cochiti Pueblo. His eyes lit up, and he started talking about books he's read, how much wisdom Native Americans have. "They're in touch with the Maker," he said, "Everything an Indian does is in a circle because the power of the world always works in circles. Have you noticed that?"

I thought about it. I think sometimes circles can be broken.

February 3, 1946

Tan and I went to see *Saddlemates* with Sunset Carson, the most fun I've had in a while. It's hard to believe, here I am watching a cowboy movie in the wide-open wild West.

We went together to the jungle on Guadalupe, enjoyed a story teller talking about real life Indians and cowboys, then Tan and I got into our own conversation. He told me about 'taking care of business' and nobody suspecting. It was after dark at the pow wow, he stayed back in the shadows where the men went to relieve themselves, waiting for the man who killed his wife, then put a knife through his heart without making a sound, just like the son of a bitch did to Nancy.

Then he put his head in his hands and cried, "Oh, God, will I ever forget?"

I didn't know what to say so didn't say anything. After a few moments, he started talking about wanting to see all 50 states – his dream trip was Florida, then up the east coast, stopping in Virginia and Pennsylvania, maybe a few weeks in Maine, then across northern US, back to Montana. He stopped and said, "I always return to Montana, no matter what happens. The drumbeat of my soul is strongest there."

I told him I felt that way about North Dakota, only just hadn't realized it before. But I can't go back, ever. He asked me why not, and I just shook my head. I don't want to talk about it.

April 7, 1946

Tan and I were sitting on the Plaza this evening, watching people, enjoying some street musicians from Peru playing panpipes and flutes, some of the happiest music I've ever heard.

Then out of nowhere, Tan told me he had a daughter. I thought I about telling him I did too, but I couldn't make the words come out.

He said me he ran away from home when he was 15. His family had a farm near Joplin, Missouri. He hitchhiked Route 66 all the way to California. He laughed and said, "You get your kicks on Route 66, you really do!

"When I got to California," he continued, "I got in with a crowd of other runaways. I met a girl, it didn't mean anything, just trying to find myself and have a good time, but she got pregnant. I was only 16 at the time. I took off, went hitchhiking up and down the state of California for about a year, but I couldn't get the girl or our baby out of my mind. So I went back, tried to do the right thing, even got a teaching degree and taught for a while. But it didn't work. I can't live tied down with so much fighting and bickering, so I left again. We keep in touch. They're living in Albuquerque, and I'll go see them before I leave.

"But Swede, I've failed as a father!"

I put my hand on his shoulder, and we both had tears in our eyes.

May 1, 1946

Saw Jan on the Plaza, barefoot, still wearing her guitar and cowgirl skirt, blond hair in pigtails under a wide-brimmed hat. She seemed glad to see me, but her smile didn't reach her eyes. I asked about the bruises on her arm. She didn't answer me.

I tried to convince her to go home, offered to help pay for a train ticket. But no, she's doing just fine, she's getting married, thanks anyway. She met a man who calls himself Durango Drifter, another musician, and he loves her.

I gave her my last $2.00. She hugged me and kissed my cheek.

May 2, 1946

Jan left this morning with Drifter.

May 7, 1946

I've made myself a shelter out of old juniper branches and yucca leaves. Plenty of flat rock for a fire pit. I've left La Fonda. It wasn't me who took that woman's purse, but I know who did. It was a set-up. Sometimes it's better to disappear.

I'll look for ranch work tomorrow.

I sit in the sun, letting it soak into my skin. Think of nothing else, just the moment, the warmth, and the writing to you. The closest to you I can feel.

lazy afternoon
old junipers
buzz with horseflies
lizard runs the shape of his tail

pockets filled
with pretty rocks
I walk the path alone

May 9, 1946

Following train tracks south of Santa Fe, headed for Lamy Ranch (heard they were hiring), and thinking of Laura, the wife I let down. Somehow today under this big New Mexico sky, I don't feel so bad.

What's done is done, and here I am. Hard to stay miserable in such a beautiful place.

Camped last night under the same sky I've admired so much during the day.

I've found a place to sit under an ancient juniper and breathe in the pine air.

While admiring the desert grasses swaying in the breeze, I notice a rusted bolt, half buried. I dig it out to put in my pocket. Small way to keep this moment alive.

May 9, 1946

Friends at Lamy Ranch, Antonio Torres, Manuel Romero, and José Maestas. Manuel told me to be careful of hanging out with Indians. He said I was an 'outsider' and didn't want to get a reputation as an Indian-lover. Said it wasn't any better than a nigger-lover, and people here need to know their place. I told him the Indians I'd met seemed like nice people.

He got a dark look in his eyes when he said, "Don't forget what I told you."

COCHITI, NEW MEXICO

June 30, 1946

The last thing I remember in Santa Fe was walking on Water Street with Tan, on our way to listen to music on the Plaza. A group of men wearing black hats pulled over their faces grabbed us, pushed us into an alley, then started beating us with baseball bats, calling us Indian lovers and white trash. Next thing I know, I'm waking up beside a campfire on the Rio Grande, an Indian woman stirring something in a pot over a fire. Tan isn't here.

The woman came toward me waving a smoking bundle of pine twigs and needles. "Protection," was all she said. Then she brought me a bowl of soup, and I was surprised how hungry I was.

July 2, 1946

Sam came to my campsite this morning. "Good to see you're getting better, Swede," he said as he put his hand on my shoulder. "But I'm sorry to tell you, your friend wasn't so lucky."

July 3, 1946

Tan was the best friend I ever had. So young, so full of life.

Deep in my soul is broken glass.

grieving
my feet walk
without me

Can a person die of sadness?

July 5, 1946

Visit from Tribal Council today, including the governor. He called me "white man with gentle face," and said, "You have shown yourself to be our friend." He went on, "But understand, we have secret and sacred traditions to protect, that we cannot share with you. Respect that, and you are welcome on our land."

July 14, 1946

Sam invited me to the pueblo's Corn Dance. What an event. Men, women, and children wearing white costumes trimmed with red and black beads and colored feathers were shaking ears of corn and dancing in perfect unity to a pulsing drumbeat.

Sam's son Cruz invited me to join the dance. I was glad to get up and move with the rhythm, be a part of their dance. I was sorry when it was over.

Was invited to Sam's home for a feast of Native America's best food, round loaves of bread baked in outdoor ovens with green chili stew, tamales, and hand-held prune pies (Cruz called them 'empanadas.')

Cruz's sister, Marie, showed me the pottery she made, hand-painted birds and corn plants on red clay. She gave me a small plate, perfect size for my satchel.

Cruz and I spent the afternoon walking the countryside around the pueblo. He pointed out a rock painting and told me I wasn't allowed to touch it. "It belongs to native people—you're not one of us."

I followed him through winding arroyos, around rocky outcroppings and sacred landmarks, in and out of juniper and piñon forests, finally to reach tall sandstone cliffs, with hundreds of hollowed-out caves and carved stone ladders. He told me reverently that this was Bandelier, the ancient home of his ancestors. We sat in cool shade, and he talked about how they lived and how they died. I could almost feel them with us.

I wrote a poem about it later.

Ancient Dwelling

they still live you know
ancestors beloved

you hear them in the quiet of
life's murmur
in cool green of
river shade
atop sunlit mesas
juniper scent baking into skin
within kiva walls
Spirit center

they tell of
caves in canyon walls
scraping scraping
obsidian tools and basalt
autumn air filled with aroma
of ground corn, baking bread

you hear
loud thumps reverberate
stone ax meets heavy beam
mano meets matate
children laugh, dogs bark

they tell of
grief and worship
death and conception
cycles of change and
continuity

you hear no
distinction between
God and government
everything is Spirit
and Spirit is everything

they pass on
knowledge, the Spirit line
like cobble rock
rounded by water
carried by the stream

August 27, 1946

I have a job – maybe the best one yet, playground aide at the elementary school. The school principal, Gloria Suina, offered it in exchange for a little house to live in behind the school and $5.00 a week. (I think Sam had something to do with it.)

I might just stay here awhile.

September 6, 1946

Hard day at school, so much fighting between the Pena Blanca kids and the Cochiti. Then a boy shouted at me, "I don't have to listen to a white man!" I said, "No, you're right, you don't," and walked away. Came home bone tired and ready to quit.

September 14, 1946

Jump rope on Cochiti playground. Surprised them with my ability to jump double Dutch and red-hot peppers. Then I twirled and had the best time I've had in a long time.

Leona, Emily, Michele, and Holly jumped as they recited the alphabet – the letter they missed was the initial of the person they were going to marry. When it was my turn, I missed on purpose on the letter L. Laura, I don't want anyone else.

Oh sweet girls, with no idea how hard life can be.

December 25, 1946 Christmas Day

Life is a cold hard shell and I'd die if I could. It's Christmas break from school, and all I want to do is stay in bed. I'm alone, a failure, and the voices in my head are constantly telling me I'm worthless, I should die. I put my hands over my ears and cry, but it doesn't do any good.

December 27, 1946

Cruz came by to see me, saw me crying, not making sense. He left and came back with a man he introduced as Joseph and said he was a Medicine Man.

Joseph sat down beside my bed, laid a bear claw and some turquoise beads on my chest, and then started talking in the most soothing voice I've ever heard. The ugly voices inside of me shut up immediately.

He talked about living in harmony with nature, that the sun represented the Creator. There are sacred mountains in each direction, and with the sun above and earth below, we have balance in our world.

I couldn't answer; I just wanted to sleep. He told me to go ahead, rest from my battles. Tomorrow would be a new day.

December 28, 1946

Spent the day walking around the arroyos, admiring the sky, and looking for pretty rocks.

January 1, 1947

Another year. Another Corn Dance. Another celebration of life and harvest. The circle forever turning, never breaking. And I'm on the outside looking in.

I was invited to Sam's home again. Mrs. Martinez served Green Chili Stew. She laughed at how quickly I said yes when she offered me a second bowl. I told her it was delicious and one of the best things I've ever eaten. She said she was glad I liked it and had Marie copy the recipe.

January 16, 1947 Dorene's Birthday

My dear baby is 14. Does she remember me?

Dusting of snow this morning. In no hurry to leave this fire. Think I'll stay home and try making Mrs. Martinez' recipe for stew.

Cochiti Green Chilé Stew

2 pounds meat, cut in small pieces
2 tablespoons lard
½ onion, chopped
4 medium potatoes, peeled and chopped
12 large green chilés, roasted, peeled, and chopped
Salt

Brown the meat in a little oil in a large deep pan. Add the onions, fry 3 – 5 minutes. Add the potatoes. When the ingredients have browned, pour off any oil. Add the chilés and salt; cover with water and boil for at least a half hour.

January 18, 1947 Hildur's Birthday

Happy birthday, Hildur, I wish I could see you one more time, let you know I'm alive, tell you I love and admire you. I may have been older than you, but you were stronger.

Remember the time we were playing pinochle, you were about twelve, and Father caught us? Remember his loud, booming voice when he yelled about the devil using idle hands? You laughed, and he got his belt. You got about five good whacks, then you looked at me and winked. Oh Hildur, if only I had your spunk. I was the one who said, "Yes, sir," and look where it got me. I couldn't do anything right and still can't.

January 31, 1947

A blue-eyed Indian boy named José brought me a robin to eat. He had a big grin when he saw my reaction, but I tasted it anyway. I was surprised by how delicious it was. One of the older boys said "Hey, you're not supposed to give him that!" When I asked why not, he said, "Because you're not one of us. It's secret." Then he said something to José I didn't understand. José just looked down.

February 3, 1947

One of the only two white girls at school was beaten by another student today, her head slammed against her desk and nose broken. Someone said it was gang-related, but I don't understand why.

February 17, 1947

A fight on the playground. Two boys, one Mexican, the other Indian, were punching each other, rolling on the ground. I grabbed the one on top and held his arms down. All I could say was, "That's enough—stop fighting!" The bell rang, and the one I was holding spit at the other and yelled "*Pachuco*, I'll meet you after school!" I said, "Boys, get along! Go to class and forget about it." As I was walking away, one of them called out, "Go f--- yourself, white man!"

February 18, 1947

Got called to principal's office. Seems I've been accused of inappropriate contact. A parent called and complained I had my arms around his son on the playground. When I told her what happened, she asked why I didn't report it. I didn't know I was supposed to. She said the parent was a board member, and she didn't have a choice. I've been dismissed. Now what? I can't do anything right.

February 20, 1947

Sam and JD came to visit this morning. Said they heard the news I was fired and asked what happened. "I tried to stop a fight," I said, "The boy went home and told his parents that I put my arms around him on the playground. I told Mrs. Suina the story, but I messed up and didn't know to make report. So it's my word against theirs. They're on the Board, and I'm a dumb Swede. Who are they going to listen to?"

JD told me not to worry, I did the right thing. Maybe so, but doing the right thing doesn't buy my groceries, and hand-outs are hard to get.

Losing my job also means I lose my house. Back under the stars for me.

February 24, 1947

I packed my satchel and bed roll, walked into the Pueblo, and went to the Governor's Office. Sat for a couple hours waiting; his secretary said he was in an important meeting. Then Delores, one of the teachers from the school, saw me and sat down next to me. "Can I help you?" she asked.

"I wanted to ask Mr. Suina if there was any work I could do for food and lodging, maybe a campsite on the reservation."

"I have something you can do," Delores said. "My father needs someone to stay with him while I'm at work, to cook and clean up after him, mostly to be there if he needs help. He doesn't see well and loses his balance, too. If you're interested, I can take you to meet him."

March 10, 1947

Staying with Mr. Martin. Such a kind and wise man, he treats me like a friend. I hold his elbow while he walks; he tells me stories.

He was a children's author. Has written over 100 books, mostly stories in rhyme. I could sit by his side for hours, listening to tales about a big-eared burro, disappearing dark horses, and weeping pine trees.

April, 4, 1947

Sorry to say, Mr. Martin's going downhill. Doesn't get out of bed much. He likes me to read to him. I was reading from a book of Indian poetry about a dying moon claiming the lives of the old and sick. He stopped me and said, "Swede, I'm old and sick. I hear the dying moon calling me."

May 5, 1947

Said good-bye to Mr. Martin.

Now that he's gone, not much for me to do around here.

Delores says I can continue to stay here. She likes my company, and I have to say, it's nice to not be alone.

May 6, 1947

Spent the day digging irrigation ditches. They've dammed up the Rio Grande east of the Pueblo to make a lake and the Governor got word to me that they'd welcome help with digging ditches. I didn't realize how hard it was to dig rocky red New Mexican soil. My back is killing me.

I mentioned to Sam what I did yesterday, digging ditches from Cochiti Lake to different fields. He shook his head, "It's a sad day, when we need to flood our sacred grounds to get more water for farming."

May 8, 1947

Someone threw a rock through the front window this morning. A note was tied to it that said, "If you know what's good for you, white man, leave our women alone."

May 9, 1947

I'm heading out in the morning. I've enjoyed my time in Cochiti, but my feet are itching to move. Plus, having an Indian girlfriend might be more trouble than it's worth.

May 10, 1947

I gave Sam this poem—

Cochiti, New Mexico

Ancient mesas
call me home,
my brothers of red earth,
souls of sibling bonding in
sacred geography

Standing tall
with piercing eye
nodding, knowing, hearing,

kindred drumbeat of
human heart

Ancient mesas
welcome me home
to dance the dance of celebration
we are the victor warriors
with the love that conquers all

Will the Circle be Unbroken?

AZTEC, NEW MEXICO

"Logic and sermons never convince,
The damp of the night
drives deeper into my soul." Walt Whitman

May 18, 1947

Set up camp south of town, surrounded by glorious sandstone canyons. First thing I did was head out to explore, walking a path on the edge of a steep cliff.

I heard what sounded like cicadas but was too busy admiring the way the sun was setting behind the golden mesas to pay attention. Then I happened to look down and see a long line of baby rattlesnakes, one after the other, all along the path, furious at me for disturbing their world.

I had nowhere else to go but back beside them again, all the way back to my camp. Either that or over the edge. I kept my eyes straight ahead and put one foot in front of the other, my heart pounding so loud I could hear it.

Didn't stay in the camp, packed up and high-tailed it out of there.

May 19, 1947

I'm camping along the Animas River in Aztec's city park, shaded, beautiful, and hopefully snake free. Dreamed last night I was being chased by snakes. Woke up in cold sweat with a sick taste in my mouth. Took me a while to get moving, but I noticed other campers nearby, one with a camp fire and coffee pot. I watched a while to see if the dark-skinned man with a braid down his back was sharing, and after I saw others bring their empty cups, I went over and ask if he knew where I could get a shower and something to eat. "Sure," he said, "there's the Good Samaritan House downtown. You can usually get a meal there, especially if you offer to do dishes."

He looked at the woman with him, she nodded her head, and then he said, "We've got some biscuits you can have, a cup of coffee, too."

The woman never spoke, but the man told me they were Navajos from Shiprock, on their way to the plaza in Santa Fe. He makes and sells silver and turquoise jewelry, and she weaves rugs. He showed me one of her rugs and said, "See the tightly woven design. Look closely, and you'll find a mistake. She always makes a mistake on purpose." I asked why, and he said, "So any bad spirits that get caught in the weaving can get away."

I thanked them for the coffee and told her the rug was beautiful; she nodded and looked at her feet.

Walking to Durango, about 40 miles so I hope to get a ride. I plan to try my hand at mining – who knows I might find gold and become a rich man after all.

DURANGO, COLORADO

May 20, 1947

My first train ride through the Rockies, a narrow gauge, I felt like a kid again. Sweet Jesus, what a display of God's creation. I've seen pictures, but never imagined this. It occurs to me, God must love me after all, to let me see this. I wonder at the thought.

I have to stop writing and dance awhile.

I open my face to Colorado's mountain sun.
I'm whole again.

May 21, 1947

Bloodthirsty mosquitos chased me back down the mountain.

May 22, 1947

Two men came up this afternoon, one dressed like a woman, saying they'd like to get to know me, asked me to supper and drinks. Something told me I didn't want to know them the way they meant, so I lied and said my wife was expecting me.

May 28, 1947

Cold night camping, woke to pain and stiffness in every muscle and joint. Made a fire and heated some water for washing and coffee. Finally, the sun came out and warmed things up and the world was good again – sky deep blue with brilliant white clouds and mountains tall and majestic.

Midday walk north of Hermosa, following a steep and winding path. I stop by the cool of a mountain stream, ripples washing my soul, and think of you, Dorene. In my heart, I'll never let you go.

May 30, 1947

Went to the train station in Durango and asked if I could work for a ticket to Silverton. The fellow behind the counter asked if I'd peel potatoes. I said I'd be happy to. I can actually board the train using the steps.

Sign says 'Mountain Trout Every Day in Dining Car.' Looking forward to those leftovers.

I must have peeled a hundred potatoes today. I never want to see another potato as long as I live. (And I never did taste any trout.) Glad to see Silverton's water tower.

SILVERTON, COLORADO

June 1, 1947

I've never seen anything like this town, surrounded by snow-covered peaks and air more fresh and clean than I ever imagined.

Got a job in the Grand Imperial Hotel, housekeeping instead of kitchen help. Like I said, I've peeled enough potatoes.

One of the other guests asked if I knew about the hotel ghost. Said someone shot himself and no one noticed. He didn't die until morning, apparently after a long night of agony. People still hear his moaning.

I'm not sure I can work here.

June 2, 1947

Left the Grand Imperial. Voices screamed from every direction. I tried not to listen, but then I had a dream about a dying man who was me. But I couldn't die. Pain ripped through me, and I woke up crying and covered with sweat.

I've made a camp next to the Animas River. I'll look for work tomorrow.

Right now, I want to listen to rippling water dance its way down the mountain.

June 3, 1947

Split firewood for a woman who introduced herself as Mrs. Ballentine. She lives on the edge of town, an elderly woman with a welcome sign in her driveway. Worked two hours. She paid me a dollar and a plate of biscuits. Said she'd appreciate it if I'd come back in a couple days and fix her back door.

June 5, 1947

Back at Mrs. Ballentine's, not going to pass up the offer of work, and those biscuits she gave me tasted like Laura's.

Mrs. Ballentine left for the post office, and I'm here alone on her front porch, drinking the ginger water she made me, eating biscuits and jam, and thinking about wife, my daughter, and the son I've never seen. The missing them, it never goes away. The beauty around me, the adventure, only helps ease the pain for the moment. There's a hole in my heart that nothing can fill.

I was enjoying the quiet when the sheriff walked up and said he doesn't believe he's seen me around before. He asked what I was doing in town. I told him I was looking for odd jobs and maybe some mining. Well, he said he's taking me in for questioning, and now I'm sitting in a jail cell in city hall, and no one's asked me a single damn question.

Seems there's been a bank robbery. Someone who matches my description, tall and thin wearing a cap over his face, robbed the clerk at gun point, which is probably a hanging offense in this town. My God, if they really think I did it, would I have been sitting in broad daylight, writing in a journal and eating biscuits?

June 7, 1947

The sheriff and his deputies caught the real bank robber, or rather shot him in an old-fashioned gun fight on Main Street. The money was found and returned, and I'm a free man.

When the sheriff let me out, he said, "Sorry about that—mistakes happen. A big coincidence, someone matching your description, and you being new in town. You're free to go, but we're not welcoming strangers right now. The silver mines in Eureka are hiring anyone willing to work. Tell them Sheriff Steve sent you."

EUREKA, COLORADO

gunfights, gambling
red lights and ladies of the night

June 8, 1947

I lasted five minutes in the mine shaft, then ran out as fast as I could. I couldn't breathe, cold hands squeezed my throat and hate-filled voices laughed in the shadows. I went to the foreman and apologized. He called me a dumb Swede, asked what I was so scared of. I shook my head, "I just can't go in there." (If I told him the mine was a long dark hole of shadows and voices, he'd know I was crazy.) He said, "Suit yourself, go find a job somewhere else."

"I can do other things for you," I told him. "I'd like to stay the summer. I can cook, wash dishes, whatever you want. I just don't want to go underground."

He looked at me like I was an idiot, then said "Ok, it just so happens I can use help with the cooking. If you want to peel potatoes for a crew of 30 every day, you're hired."

I know I promised myself no more potato peeling, but it's better than that long dark hole. I can peel potatoes and pan for gold and silver in my spare time. I might get lucky yet.

June 23, 1947

Other miners invited me into town. I should have known better.

In a poker game next to us, the man winning had an ace of spades fall out of his sleeve and was shot dead on the spot. The man who did the shooting looked at me and asked what I was staring at. I said excuse me and got up to leave. He stood up, shoved my shoulder, and asked, "Where you going? Consequences of cheating too much for you?" When I didn't answer, he called me "delicate"; his friends thought that was hilarious and started in too. Sissy, momma's boy, not right. Everyone laughing and pointing. Good time for the sheriff to walk in. I wasted no time leaving.

July 4, 1947

A couple of the guys invited me to the Fourth of July celebration in Silverton, something to remember, a festival of pie and patriotism, fireworks in mountain majesty. I helped Mrs. Ballentine set up her booth of baked goods and jams and was rewarded with a piece of the best rhubarb pie I've ever tasted.

July 24, 1947

I've found a log in a convenient spot for sitting.
Lupines wave while baby oak leaves quiver in the breeze

Dorene, I don't know if you'll ever read my journals. I hope someday you do.

Father called me a dreamer, a good worker for a while but didn't stick with anything. He said I'd be good for nothing if I didn't change my ways.

Well, he was right, I don't amount to much. I'm not good enough to be your daddy.

September 4, 1947

on the canvas of my soul –
rabbit brush, desert marigold
a sky of mountain blue

September 7, 1947

It's a good time for me to leave. Nights are getting cold, and I'm heading south, where winters are more to my liking.

TAOS, NEW MEXICO

September 12, 1947

Sleeping under a railroad trestle with other nameless travelers. It's been a while since I've gone through garbage for food, but it might come to that. I'm so hungry, it's all I can think about. I'll try one more time to find work, but then so help me God, I'll eat what I can get.

After knocking on half a dozen doors and no luck, I saw a group of Indian women with a food stand. I went up and asked if they I had anything I could do for something to eat. They all just looked at me like who did I think I was, then the oldest one said, "You clean up chicken shit?" The rest laughed, but I didn't waste any time saying, "Yes, Ma'am" You should have seen their faces. Then she nodded and said, pointing with her chin, "About a mile north of town, follow the signs for Taos Pueblo, then turn right just past the plaza. You'll see chicken houses. You clean them out for me, and I'll be home at lunch time and feed you."

I thanked her, headed out and found the chicken houses. I wasn't sure I could do it, but the smell took away some of my appetite. I had the buildings cleaned the best I could in about an hour and a half. When she came home and saw what I'd done, she said, "You sit here under this tree, I'll be right back."

She brought me more food than I could eat and said, "You can take the left-overs. You did a better job than I thought you would."

September 17, 1947

I've found a job at Red Chili Tavern, washing dishes, scrubbing floors, cleaning the toilet, for two dollars a day and all the table scraps nobody sees me take. From 11:00 in the morning to 8:00 at night.

Still sleeping under the railroad trestle, but I tell myself, this is only temporary. As soon as I can save some money, I'm heading out.

September 22, 1947

Walking though the old part of town, I saw a sign that said 'Home of Kit Carson, Museum and Library' and decided it'd be worth a dollar to see. I was met at the door by a tour guide, who happened to be a descendant of Carson's. The man spent the next hour showing me the house and telling stories. The rest of the afternoon I sat in the courtyard shade imagining what it was like exploring wild frontiers, rescuing ladies in distress, riding against the wind.

To Kit Carson, wherever you are

I met your descendant
his wavy red hair and steely blue eyes
said to come from you
he plays your part, you know
re-enacting the legend

some say you were a scoundrel
cold-hearted, vindictive
but I found this man a gentleman
unassuming, upright
with a simple, honest smile

so I choose to believe the best
you must have been
more good than bad
your word as sure as the sunrise
I saw it in his eyes

I looked down and saw a dog staring up at me. Maybe beagle, mostly mutt. I patted her head and talked to her and then couldn't get rid of her. Unless somebody claims her, I guess she's mine. She followed me back to camp, and I named her Suzie.

September 24, 1947

Stopped by the jungle for news and free food (someone said elk in the stew.) Suzie and I both enjoyed the meal (I didn't let anyone see me feeding her.)

Heard the oil rigs were hiring in Texas. Sounds like just the adventure I'm looking for.

TEXHOMA, OKLAHOMA

October 1, 1947

Staying in a dugout. All I have is hard bread.

Oh God, what is this hell I've come to? Air black and thick with blowing grit, breathing dust through my skin. Will it ever stop?

Lord Jesus, if you're real and love me the way Father said, then please, help me, please.
My soul is black, I have no words.

Oklahoma wind
I too
am dust

October 3, 1947

Got a week's job working at Cattle Congress, washing dishes and cleaning, only 50 cents a day, but the food is good, and I get a bed in one of the barns. Texhoma might not be such a God-forsaken place after all.

BORGER, TEXAS

October 10, 1947

Life is good mostly – I can go about anywhere I want and find work. Here I am, in a place I've never been, and just got hired to work on an oil rig.

A man in the diner was calling for roustabouts for Phillips Petroleum. I told him I was interested. He looked me up and down, then shook my hand and said, "Nice to meet you. I'm John Noble, foreman of several rigs here. We're short of laborers. Are you interested?"

I nodded yes, even though I had no idea what exactly a laborer did on an oil rig. I figured I could learn. He went on to say I'd make $1.25 an hour, paid every Friday, and could have a bunk in one of the row houses. Doesn't get much better than that.

October 12, 1947

Roustabout is a good word for it. I go here and there, doing what needs to be done. Today I dug ditches, yesterday I laid pipe. Tomorrow I'm peeling damn potatoes.

October 13, 1947

Worked in the cooking tent with a young man named Benny, a friendly talker. We had a contest to see who peeled the most potatoes, but we're not sure who won. It helped the day go by.

He talked about the dangers of working on an oil rig, the explosions, the heavy equipment, the derrick monkey boards 80 feet above the ground. He said a guy fell off last year, his own fault, walking around with his safety rope not attached.

Maybe roustabouts don't make much, but he said he'd much rather dig ditches than work that high off the ground or get his face blown off, just to make some big shot in Houston rich.

Then he got on the subject of the town of Borger, all the murders and crime, gambling and gangsters. He said that during prohibition this town was under martial law, the governor called in the Texas Rangers. They rounded up all the bootleggers, prostitutes, drug dealers, and card sharks and hauled them across the border. Maybe it helped for a while, but didn't last long, and the town was just as lawless as before. Turns out the mayor's best friend was one of the crime bosses.

October 19, 1947

Pay day, and what'd I do? Went to Borger with Benny and his brother Travis. Dumbest thing I ever did. I'm broke again, and my head is killing me. I know those slot machines were rigged, and I should never drink more than two beers. Travis and Benny probably aren't feeling too well this morning either.

The worst part, I got approached by another shady-looking character who wanted me to run errands to Mexico. I asked him if it was legal. I thought he took too long to answer, so I said, "No, thanks." (I learned that lesson in New Orleans.) He grabbed me by the collar and said he had my name and there were ways to influence me.

I'm going back to bed.

October 21, 1947

Digging ditches all day is hard work. If it wasn't for Benny beside me and his storytelling, I don't know if I'd do it. But then I do the math and figure if I can make it to the end of the month, I'll have close to $100. I'd feel like a rich man, relax and enjoy living for a change.

Benny got on the subject of digging horizontal pipeline for natural gas, called it 'fracking'. Said it was first done in the 1860's, and Standard Oil has started doing it again to increase production. "Don't you believe everything you hear. It doesn't hurt anything, doesn't pollute drinking water or poison the soil, if it's done right." I didn't know anything about it so didn't say anything, just nodded. He went on, "People just like stirring things up, and they'll believe what they want to."

Or there's people like me, who try to stay out of it and don't like debate. I'd rather write poetry about the shapes and shadows in the landscape when the sun sets after a long day, than pretend I'm smarter than I am and know anything for certain.

October 22, 1947

One of the biggest challenges here is getting clean. Oil is in the air, thick and black, coating my skin; then the dry panhandle dirt sticks like a coat of paint. The only shower is a hose and a bar of soap.

And I'm breathing the damn stuff—probably coating the inside of my lungs too. Counting down the days to the end of the month.

October 23, 1947

Benny's conversation today was about a haunted house in Borger. The story is that back in '17, a man accidently shot and killed his sister in a library, and he starved himself to death as punishment. Benny's sister Alice went there yesterday and swore that she heard a man crying. Benny asked if I wanted to go there sometime. I said, "No way in hell."

October 25, 1947

Saturday night and this Swede's staying right here.

I never worked this hard in my entire life. I fall into bed at night with nothing to write about and nothing to remember, just work and noise and hard red clay.

At least I have Suzie—glad to see me at the end of the day. I think the best friend I ever had. She doesn't care if I'm worthless, she loves me anyway.

October 29, 1947

I've worked about 12 hours a day, 10 days in a row. I'm about at the end of my rope.

October 30, 1947

Machines so loud, I couldn't hear what Benny was saying. Then I heard the word 'crushed' and saw them carrying a stretcher to an ambulance.

Within 5 minutes, everyone was back to work like nothing happened.

November 1, 1947

I was getting ready to head out, when I got called to the sheriff's office. He wanted to know if I'd been in Borger on the night of October 19 and asked if was I approached by a tall thin man wearing a grey suit and black fedora, with a long scar down the side of his face? I nodded yes. Then he wanted me to describe the conversation. I told him the man didn't give me his name, just asked if I wanted some easy money. I told him no. and I haven't gone back into Borger since.

"He's been found with a bullet hole in the back of his head. The word's going around that you snitched on him. I'd be careful if I was you."

Why does trouble always find me?

November 2, 1947

Benny came to my bunk about 3:00 this morning and shook my shoulder, "Wake up, wake up! You got a big problem. One of the mayor's thug men has pointed the finger at you for blabbing about the drug dealing. You need to disappear quick."

He said to head toward Houston, get a ranch job, and stay out of towns like Borger. He sure as heck got that right.

Made a sling for Suzie from an old blanket so she can ride on my back. Suzie girl, we're on the road again.

ABBOT, TEXAS

November 3, 1947

Hopped off the train to find a meal. Noticed some boys had climbed to the top of the town water tower. One of them, a red-head with freckles and a bandana around his forehead, told me to watch him while he hung upside-down by one leg. I told him I wasn't impressed, and he called me a name I didn't catch. I told him I was looking for someone to do a favor and would pay a nickel if he would help. He came right down, stuck out his hand, and said, "Hi, I'm Willie."

I introduced myself as Dakota Swede, a traveling worker looking for a job. He spit and said, "You won't tell my grandma what we were doing?" I nodded and he offered me a handshake.

To make a long story short, I ended up cleaning his grandmother's gutters for the best cornbread and pinto beans I ever tasted. I impressed Willie by telling him stories about hobos and riding the rails. He told me to stop by again, he hopes to be a traveling musician someday, just don't tell his grandma.

TEAGUE, TEXAS

November 5, 1947

Hopped off the train as it slowed for Teague. Found a jungle by the water tower. No soup pot but there's a house up the street that offers free food. I asked about finding work and was told I could try the hotel next to the train station, or the brick factory south of town. I decided to find food first.

The house was easy to find, the only one with a shiny metal roof. I went to the back door and knocked. A woman in her 50's with curly red hair and painted eyebrows, invited me into a screened porch. She said to wait, the stew was still stewing. Then she pointed to Suzie, "Your dog has to stay outside."

I pulled out the book of Native American poems Tan gave me back in Santa Fe, but before I could start reading, one of the other travelers introduced himself as Hobo Harry and then wouldn't shut up. Went on and on about traveling with a carnival, all the tricks he's played and the jokes he's told. Finally, the woman came back with several bowls of steaming stew on a tray and introduced herself as Schotzie Langdon. "My real name is Barbara, but my husband started calling me Schotzie during the war. It's German for sweetheart.

"Come back next Saturday night and you'll meet my husband Homer. He plays the banjo; I play the fiddle. All musicians, poets, storytellers, vagabonds, and misfits are invited to come. We get together once a month and celebrate a good time."

Harry laughed, "What about the hooch?" Schotzie scowled and said, "And I can show you the door." That shut him up.

After a meal of the most interesting stew I've had (someone said squirrel and possum), I went to the Teague Hotel and offered to work in exchange for food, a hot bath, and a place to sleep. The owner said I had an honest face, and it just so happened, he could use me.

November 6, 1947

Well that didn't work out. It seems I resemble some guy on a Wanted Poster in Waco. I overheard the boss's wife on the phone with the sheriff and decided it might be a good idea to leave.

Walked out to brick plant west of town, through the colored part of town. (In Teague, whites live east of the railroad tracks; coloreds live west.) Just so happened, they were hiring. Four dollars a day is good money. If I can stay at Scottie's, I think I'll stick around Teague for a while.

November 8, 1947

Enjoyed the party at Homer and Scottie's—everyone happy and laughing. Their son Bobby and nephew Gil got everyone dancing with their guitar playing, and I joined right in.

Gil and Bobby left early through the back door when they thought no one was looking.

Lying on a cot on the Langdon porch tonight, counting stars and wondering if Doreen is looking at the same sky. Does she think of me? Does she cry?

November 9, 1947

Schotzie was fit to be tied this morning. Gil and Bobby are in the county jail for vandalism. Seems like after they left the party last night, they went out drinking and were caught painting on the town's water tower, something about Waco's cheerleaders.

Schotzie says they can sit there a while.

November 12, 1947

Working at the brick plant, mostly loading and unloading, backbreaking work, but the money's good, the crew is friendly, and I make enough to pay Schotzie a weekly rent. I hope to stay at least tile Spring. Schotzie says Suzie can sleep on the porch.

Gil and Bobby are working here too. Schotzie says they've got to work out their bail money or she'll take it off their hides.

November 13, 1947

If it wasn't for the boys, this job would be more work than it's worth. They have a good time no matter what they're doing. Singing a Hank Williams song or reciting Hamlet's soliloquy, they're so entertaining, I forget my aching back.

November 14, 1947

I enjoy the daily walk through Colored Town. Children run after me (I bring penny candy), and old folks call from porch rocking chairs, "Hello Mister, beautiful day we're having."

November 16, 1947

Homer's got me started whittling. I'm surprised how much I enjoy it. Making little pinewood animals. I try to do a different one every night, each about two inches tall and looking as close to real as I can get.

November 24, 1947 Thanksgiving Day

bright autumn
nature's last melody

December 25, 1947 Christmas Day

Your 13th Christmas, your 10th without me. Oh Dorene, if you only knew how much I miss you.

Went down to Colored Town to take my mind off sadness. Brought the animals I whittled to give to the children.

January 16, 1948 Dorene's birthday

You probably don't remember the sock dolls your Aunt Imogene made for your third birthday. You carried that family of dolls around in your wagon and talked to them like they were real. That's how I see you in my mind, three years old. Then I think, you're 14, and I'm not with you.

I'd die if I could.

January 18, 1948 Hildur's birthday

Mother's death was probably harder for Hildur than me. She was only 2 when it happened, but she always seemed so sad and lonely after that, playing by herself in the attic, talking to her toys. I don't know if I ever heard her laugh.

January 24, 1948

In bed with double pneumonia. Schotzie called Dr. Stephens from Waco.

Schotzie decided Suzie could come in and stay with me.

February 9, 1948

Schotzie brought me hot tea with a shot of moonshine. Says I better get well quick, this isn't some damn flop house—I've got rent to pay.

I promised I'd give her all I owe when I get better and go back to work. Now all I want to do is sleep.

February 16, 1948

Schotzie said she's made arrangements for me to go to her brother Tom's out in the country. He had a bed set up in the corner of his barn I could use. "I need this room for paying boarders. Money doesn't grow on trees you know."

God, I got to snap out of this.

April 7, 1948

Gil brought a book of Emily Dickinson 's poems this morning. He offered to read to me and stayed for more than an hour. After he left, I got up and went outside to feel the sun shine on my face.

April 9, 1948

Gil invited me up to the house to meet his Uncle Wayne. On the way, he told me his uncle hasn't been right since the Battle of the Bulge. Didn't come out of his house for a year, has been in and out of the mental hospital. Gets a shock treatment, then he's ok for a while.

Wayne and I made eye contact, and I saw something I recognized.

April 10, 1948

Visited Wayne today. I did all the talking at first. I don't know why, but I ended up telling him all about Laura and Dorene, and even Gerald, the son I've never met. I told him about the insane asylum in Iowa. Once I started, I couldn't stop until I got it all out.

He didn't look up when he started talking, but I bet he talked for an hour, telling about the war, the noise and the smell of dying, the dark hand that chokes him in the night, and the dreams that leave him shaking.

Neither of us spoke again except to say good night.

April 12, 1948

Back at Wayne's. A tin of dominoes beside him, he asked if I'd like to play. Of course I did. We played several games, and I have no idea who won. He invited me to have supper with him, saltines and a can of sardines.

Lead Belly on the radio singing "Cotton Fields." He asked if I wanted to try it. He played the washboard, gave me some spoons to join in.

We're going to be all right.

April 16, 1948

Gil's dad offered me a job on the cotton gin starting Monday. I'm ready to work, tired of these empty pockets and people taking care of me.

April 19, 1948

I work a machine that separates cotton seeds from fiber. A monotonous job—and loud. A steam-powered whistle pierces my ears every time I add more cotton. I hate to ask Mr. Langdon for a job change, but this is not for me.

April 20, 1948

Mr. Langdon said beggars can't be choosy. I can either run the machine or hit the road. He suggested stuffing my ears with cotton. I'll try it—don't like to travel broke. Or owing people money—Schotzie's got some room and board coming.

April 24, 1948

Suzie took off today, thought I'd lost her, walked around the neighborhood at least five times calling her name, but no sign of her. I came back to the barn with a heavy heart, then she showed up at supper time. Damn dog. Why do I care?

April 25, 1948

In the Langdon kitchen, I stare at the pattern made by dried mud and see the face of a woman, her mouth shaped in an O, like she was surprised by more pain than she ever imagined.

Mrs. Langdon gave me a couple buckets of food to take to Colored Town. "Just don't tell my husband," she whispered.

On my way back from Colored Town, a man stepped out into the middle of the road with a shotgun and called me a nigger lover. He hit me in the stomach with the butt of his gun. I fell to the ground, he kicked me again—at least ten times, and said he better not see me again.

I didn't disagree with him, and here I am, riding in a box car. Suzie and I are heading south.

CRABB, TEXAS

April 27, 1948

Hopped off the train at Crabb Switch this morning, just south of Houston. Heard about the jungle here, a steady supply of mulligan, friendly locals, and a fair-minded town marshal.

Turns out everyone's on the look-out for an escapee from the pen who killed a guard with a pocket knife and got away. Has a hobo name, Jack Roller, so they're thinking he might show up here. People in the jungle are keeping their eyes down and not making much conversation.

Not everyone seeking a bowl of stew and warm fire is an honest-to-goodness hobo, a working man trying to get by.

I've been watching three women here in the jungle. They're staying close together and by the fire.

Some people you can trust, but most you better not.

May 1, 1948

They captured the convict, took him to the state prison in Austin.

The three women made mulligan and campfire biscuits, introduced themselves as Cotton-eyed Kathy, Flagstaff Fritz, and Shantytown Sue. Said they were farm workers who traveled together from job to job. They especially enjoy organizing jungle events, and since the convict's been arrested, they decided the mood was right, and life was something to celebrate. They each recited a poem and then invited any of the rest of us to share something – I recited my "Gladstone" and "Ancestors Beloved" poems. A few others came after me. Fog Man played his guitar and sang a song about a blue-eyed blond who stole his heart. Someone got a fiddle out, then another guitar, and then folks started dancing. Most fun in a long time.

Fog quoted another hobo he called Steam Train Maury Graham, "Friends are the sum total of a hobo's wealth."

I'm a wealthy man tonight.

RICHMOND, TEXAS

May 3, 1948

In the morning, I'll find out if it's true that there's plenty of work here. In the meantime, I've found a nice camp spot in a forest, lakes and marshes all around, and Suzie and I are going exploring.

May 4, 1948

Wonderful day to be alive – sunshine most pleasant, alone with my journal and thoughts, sitting on the bank of Brazos River, Suzie beside me. I plan to spend the day fishing.

Texas Bayou

symphony of sounds
just listen
octaves of birdsong
echo across swales and sloughs
oxbow lakes and marshes

hushed audience of
moss-draped oaks
twisted sycamores and noble
cottonwoods
stand in ovation

while mud-colored alligators
watch with one eye and
a strutting crane
stretches out its neck
and waits

May 5, 1948

Drizzly day, changed my mind about looking for work. Hitchhiked to the public library instead. Found an interesting book about Richmond's climate. Their record low is 51°. I might stay here awhile.

May 6, 1948

Decided it's time to look for work—free food is easy to find, but sleeping on the ground is getting old.

May 7, 1948

Went to Drabek's cotton rarm about three miles south of Rosenburg (town next to Richmond) and offered to help in the fields. Mr.

Drabek said, "Sure, hoe all you want. Pay is $2.00 a day." I asked about a place to sleep. He said I was welcome to stay in the barn.

May 9, 1948

I believe I walked through heaven on earth this morning, through a forest filled with flowers—I asked a stranger what flowers were.

Red Buckeye, poetry in nature.

May 21, 1948 Laura's birthday

I admire the yellow roses, climbing into the trees and filling the forest, just as the Red Buckeye's did two weeks ago.

Laura, I'd make you a bouquet for you if I could.

June 10, 1948

Looks like Suzie's having pups. Good Lord, now what I am going to do?

June 11, 1948

I walked into town to do some shopping and look for a cardboard box for Suzie.

June 20, 1948 Father's Day

My grandfather's name was Martin Nelson. My father was Martin's son so that's where the name Martinson comes from. If we were still in Sweden, my last name would be Larson—yours would be Reubensdotter.

June 23, 1948

Handouts are plentiful here so I'm only working when I have to. I spent the afternoon in the library reading poetry. I found a book by e. e. cummings and cried when I read his poem "i carry your heart with me (i carry it in my heart)." Dorene, I think he wrote it for us.

June 24, 1948

Barefoot in sand at Surfside Beach, Texas. Oh Lord, if I could just stop time and stay right here.

old beach chairs
faded blue
one tipped over

June 27, 1948

I write my name
in dust of dreams
old books on forgotten shelf

I'm sitting on the bank of Brazos River again, my writing bench, where I can sit and watch the muddy river's lazy flow and let my pen write whatever it wants.

cold gray day
vultures watch from
moss-shrouded trees

Funny thing what a person remembers. Hands, for example. I can still picture everyone's hands – my father's big and thick, Aunt Mary's long and graceful, Mormor's cracked and callused.

July 7, 1948

Suzie's pups born today, four squealing wiggling balls of white and brown fur. I don't know what I'm going to do with them, but I'll think about that later. For now, I can't stop watching them, I feel like I've got a family again. I've named them Dixie, Daisy, Delilah, and Duke.

July 16, 1948

I've spent the last week doing odd jobs for Mrs. Drabek, painted the back porch, dug a new flower bed. She pays me with food, left overs for me and table scraps for Suzie.

July 18, 1948

Went to a Lutheran church in Richmond this morning with the Drabek's, thought it'd be good for me, but then the music started, and I remembered my childhood and the family I failed. I left out the back door.

July 27, 1948

Spending most of my time fishing. Mr. Drabek says if I'm going to stay in his barn, the least I can do is bring him some fish. Sounds like a deal to me. And the Brazos is full of fish – three kinds of bass and catfish too.

August 2, 1948

I haven't been writing because I read over my journals and my writing is stupid and no one will ever care so why bother?

August 4, 1948

Back in Drabek's fields, hand-harvesting early cotton. A woman pulls her baby behind her on a cotton sack, singing to it as she works.

August 9, 1948

I've got four puppies following me everywhere, running around my feet. The kids in the cotton fields are delighted, but Mr. Drabek's given me a gunny sack and says they have to go.

I took the sack but knew I couldn't do it. I might be a piece of shit, but I'm not that low.

I was trying to think of what I could do, hide the dogs somehow, but then Mrs. Drabek came to the barn and said, "Don't worry, I'll find homes for them. The sharecropper kids will be glad to have them."

August 10, 1948

Hobo in the jungle was talking about Vicksburg, Mississippi, said all the old mansions were something to see and jobs were everywhere. Decided to check it out myself. Two weeks of picking cotton has taught me what a 'cotton-picking minute" is (the longest damn minute there is).

On the Road Home

VICKSBURG, MISSISSIPPI

August 17, 1948

This is some city. Spent the morning wandering the streets. Found the public library, tied Suzie in the shade and went inside. Looked through a picture book of historic homes. My favorite was the Anchuca, Choktaw for 'happy home.' A beautiful mansion, but according to the history, the home wasn't happy—the father lost everything after slavery was abolished, two of their children died of measles, and the mother had a nervous breakdown and never recovered.

Our house in North Dakota looked happy from the outside, too.

August 19, 1948

Got hired for a day's worth of gardening at the Anchuca House, of all places, for lunch and 50 cents an hour.

I left after about 30 minutes. So much yelling and fighting coming from the house, glass breaking, doors slamming. I walked away without getting paid.

Found a jungle with a sign nailed to a tree, 'Welcome to the Magnolia State, a good place for free food, a place to camp, and folks who don't ask questions.

August 20, 1948 Father's Day

Some of the best memories from my childhood are the family dances. After almost every get-together, we danced. I remember one 4th of July when Father invited everyone from church and all the neighborhood for a picnic. There were probably 75 people in our yard that day (and at least 10 tables of food.) Uncle Per Erik pushed his hand-made pipe organ from the living room into the yard, Uncle Gus played the fiddle, and Uncle Otto played a tenor horn. The music was lively and light, and we danced until dark.

I remember my aunts trying to teach me the Slängpolska, but too much spinning for me. I'd get so dizzy I could barely stand. They'd clap their hands and spin some more.

August 24, 1948

A man in the jungle with one leg, walked with a wooden peg and looked like a pirate. He stood on a box and offered anyone a job who'd come to his new restaurant in Pensacola, Florida. Said he was looking for cooks, dishwashers, waitresses, and bus boys, and starting pay was two dollars a day with tips, leftovers, and raises in pay if we stayed. I wonder why he's looking for workers in a hobo jungle two states away, but keep my mouth shut.

August 25, 1948

I've worked enough odd jobs to buy travel supplies and extra food. I've decided to put off my trip north till next spring. I want to see Florida – going to look up Mr. Peg Leg after all – can't hurt to try.

PENSACOLA, FLORIDA

August 28, 1948

Peg Leg is still out of town, but I've found work in Gulf Breeze on a fishing boat; bay scallops, oysters, blue crabs, and shrimp. We take our catch to Saunders Fish House and get paid a percentage of the catch. Yes, this is the life for me.

Dorene, how I wish you were here. I'd love to show you this, walk with you on the beach, picking up seashells and wading the shoreline waves.

August 29, 1948

Went looking for the jungle, found two hobo signs near the water tower. One was a circle with two lines which means "Get out fast;" the other was two interlocked circles representing handcuffs. In other words, hobos are hauled off to jail here. I didn't have to think about it. I walked away from there like I had somewhere to go.

August 30, 1948

Living on a boat takes some getting used to, standing on a floor that's always moving, having to grab hold at any minute to keep from falling. But I'm rocked to sleep every night, and every sunrise and set is a glorious site to see.

September 4, 1948

Took a gallon of oysters to a place called Tan Yard, a waterfront neighborhood of Spanish and French creole. Musicians on every corner, bright colors everywhere, children ragged and barefoot playing in the street. Maybe it's different after dark, but this morning, it was a happy place.

September 6, 1948

What a day—when I went to the Tan Yard this morning, I heard a woman screaming and a young boy came running and cried, "Help, Mister, my momma needs help! Sister went for Ms. Lucy, but they're not back, and Momma says the baby's not coming right. You've got to help. Please!"

My first thought was to turn and walk away, but the woman's screams changed my mind. I've helped with calves before. I knew I had to do it.

Sure enough, the baby was backwards. I told the boy to get his mother something to bite on, then go outside. With eyes as big as quarters, he said "Yes, sir, thank you, sir."

As soon as the door closed behind him, I reached inside the woman, turned the baby, and then guided it out as gently as I could. A beautiful brown-skinned baby girl, crying and plump. I was just tying the cord when the midwife came. I told her she just missed it. "You're a God-send!" she said as she took the baby from me.

The woman could barely talk, but she thanked me and said I could name the baby.

"I had a daughter once, I named her Dorene Mae. That's the prettiest name I know." "Then this baby's Dory Mae, and I'll tell her someday about you, the stranger who helped her be born."

As I was leaving the Tan Yard, I saw a one-eyed black man sitting on an overturned bucket, playing spoons, and singing "Oh Susanna." I gave him a quarter.

September 8, 1948

I'm the dumbest Swede there is. Got a new job for Patty's Fishing, and first thing I do is fall in the water trying to tie the damn sail. Went under so many times before they got to me, now my lungs feel like they're made of cement, my head is about to explode, and they're taking me to a hospital in Pensacola.

September 10, 1948

Feeling better. They drained my lungs and let me sleep for two days. I'm ready to get moving.

September 13, 1948

Went back to Patty's Fishing; they told me they weren't hiring. In other words, "Hit the road, Jack."

Sleeping in a tar paper shack near 17th Avenue Bridge. Mosquitos the size of dragonflies and all hungry.

September 15, 1948

Went to library to do some reading. I asked the librarian if she knew of a mission, or somewhere I could get a shower and a bed.

"There's the Catholic Church, St. Joe's down in Tan Yard," she said. "If that doesn't work, come back. I know someone with a houseboat that's sitting empty. You might be able to work something out with him."

I thanked her and headed to the church. I knew exactly where it was. The priest said, "Sorry, we can offer you a shower and a meal, but our beds are full."

So I'm under the bridge again, swatting mosquitos, and wondering why in God's name I'm alive.

September 16, 1948 My Birthday

Went back to the library to ask about that houseboat. She said, "Wait a minute, let me make a phone call." She came back in about five minutes and said it was ok, her husband said I could use their boat.

"It needs some repair that you could do in exchange for rent until you find something else. You don't wear the same size my husband, but I'm sure we can find you some clothes."

She introduced herself as Dorothy. Said if I was interested, her husband Danny would come to take me to the boat.

I thanked her and told her today was my birthday, and she's given me a good gift.

She laughed and said, "We know what you did for that women in the Tan Yard, we're happy to help."

September 17, 1948

I don't know where she got them, but Mrs. Dorothy found a pair of work pants, and two clean shirts.

All Danny wanted me to do was put some tar on the roof. Took me less than an hour.

September 21, 1948

I got hired at the San Carlos Hotel and offered a bed in the basement, but when I asked about Suzie, they said no dogs allowed. So Suzie and I are staying right here in Danny's house boat.

September 25, 1948

I spent the morning transplanting roses, pruning trumpet vines. Dorothy invited me in for lunch, a cold Pepsi and the best sandwich ever. She called it a muffelatta, served on a large round bread loaf and layered with cheeses, meats, and an olive salad. She showed me the recipe.

Muffelatta

1 quart broken green olives
1 cup chopped celery
1 medium onion, chopped
1 carrot in ¼" pieces
4 cloves garlic, minced
2 teaspoons oregano
1 juiced lemon and ½ its rind, grated
¼ cup olive oil
¼ cup vinegar

Mix and soak overnight. Serve at room temperature.

For sandwich, layer bread with cheese, salami, and ham. Spread with Muffelatta.

September 27, 1948

Peg Leg has finally returned from wherever he was, and I've got job at his restaurant. Working in the kitchen, peeling potatoes and washing dishes, not exactly the job he offered, but next time there's an opening for wait staff, he says the job's mine, and he'll split the tips 50–50.

October 8, 1948

One thing I can say about Mr. Peg Leg, he serves good food—trains the cooks himself, and the place is packed every night. I won't be running out of work.

Meals don't come with his payment plan after all, but I eat the extra when he's not looking. No sense throwing away good food.

October 12, 1948

Under a table at Peg's, listening to hell unleashed, I never imagined a hurricane was so loud. Voices are screaming in my head. I hear glass shattering somewhere, and I realize the glass is in me, and I'm a broken man, ready to die.

October 16, 1948

I stop to admire colors
and sounds of the beach

listen to the waves
gently sweep the shore

Learning to crab – take a chicken neck tied to a string and a scoop net – dip into salt water stream surrounded by weeds. Traps work too.

flags flew at half-mast today plane crash on Naval base and everyone killed

November 11, 1948

The sky is a gray wool blanket.

Watching the Veteran's Day Parade today in Pensacola, a celebration of America with marching bands and waving flags, I noticed a man standing behind me, with his hat down over his face. When the mayor's car went by, the mayor and his wife smiling and waving, the man rushed by yelling "Power to the people!" and started shooting.

Suzie tore after him, barking like she was going to tear him apart. Someone tackled him to the ground. The police showed up, one of the officers thumped his head with a Billy club, and no one got hurt.

November 25, 1948 Thanksgiving Day

I've been invited to Tan Yard for a Thanksgiving feast at Manuel and his wife Gabriela's (the couple who had the baby girl.) Crawfish pie, jambalaya, seafood gumbo, boiled peanuts, and bread pudding. First time for everything, and I have to say, I enjoyed every bite.

December 25, 1948 Christmas Day

Went down to Tan Yard with pockets full of penny candy, then to the mission for their Hobo Holiday Feast, mulligan with a lot of seafood and spice. I feel like a king.

I met another poet today, who told me about a group in Pensacola Beach that meets every other Friday night. They call themselves the Drowsy Poets, sometimes reading and reciting until 3 or 4 o'clock in the morning.

December 31, 1948 New Year's Eve

Can't think of any place I'd rather spend New Year's Eve than on the beach with other writers. We shared our poems around a bonfire and talked about life until dawn.

I especially enjoyed Charlie, a white-haired man who wrote about World War II. His poetry took me to the battlefield and made me glad I wasn't there.

He said he enjoyed my poems of the open road, said I made him want to be a hobo. I told him the hobo life wasn't all adventure and excitement. The open road has plenty of potholes.

January 1, 1949 New Year's Day

Invited to Danny and Dorothy's for a traditional New Year's Day meal, black-eyed peas and ham hock. After dinner, Danny got his Road Atlas, and we spent the rest of the afternoon talking about places we've been, places we'd like to go back to, and places we never want to see again.

January 16, 1949 Dorene's 16th birthday

I have a hard time imagining you any older than three, the age I last saw you. There's nothing but pain in my heart, Dorene. Pain where our love should be.

Went to the poets' meeting tonight and read the e.e. cumming's poem that he could have written for us, "i carry your heart," then embarrassed myself by crying in front of everyone.

January 18, 1949 Hildur's Birthday

Father didn't let Hildur finish high school after all—said he needed help on the farm. Maybe more to it than that, but it was a sad time for my sister. It wasn't long after that she ran away with Ernest.

January 19, 1949

I told Dorothy about the Drowsy Poets and found out she writes poetry too. We shared favorite poems for at least an hour this afternoon. She said I have a gift and someday, she'll tell people she met me. I think she's the one with gift - her poems smile and tell me everything's going to be all right.

January 20, 1949

I've about had it with Mr. Peg Leg, or maybe he's about had it with me. I can't do anything right, and he watches me like a hawk. I think I've worked here long enough.

Said good-bye to Danny and Dorothy. She wrapped some muffelattas for the road.

PANAMA CITY, FLORIDA

January 25, 1949

I've got a job with Paradise Amusements, taking care of ponies, setting up and taking down the shows, running rides, taking tickets. In other words, I'm now a 'carnie.' I wonder what Father would say?

We're sleeping in tents in an open field next to Panama City.

One thing about working with a carnival, I won't have much time to feel sorry for myself. Worked all day yesterday, just setting up. Not sure I want to get too friendly with the other carnies. They're a rough-looking bunch.

January 26, 1949

A young boy about twelve is working with me, doing the same jobs as the rest of us.

I asked him about his family. He said he didn't have one, none that he claimed anyway. He told me he ran away three months ago, his daddy died last year, and his mother was a drunk who wanted him to do everything, all the outside chores and inside housework too. "I couldn't take it anymore. All she cares about is her bottle and her boyfriends. Well, they can have her."

He said he had an older sister who ran off two years ago and they haven't seen her since, and a brother in state prison. "So it was just me and mom and a different boyfriend every other week. I've got my life ahead of me. I want to enjoy it."

He said he went to a carnival one night in Natchez and decided that was the life for him. He offered to work, and they hired him no questions asked. He's been with them ever since, seeing a new town every week and working like a man. "I'm saving money, and I've got a future now."

I just shook my head and said, "Be careful, son. This world's not always friendly."

He grinned and said, "I already know that. I'm Tommy, by the way."

January 27, 1949

I'm sitting outside under a star-filled sky, the only sounds are the horses and cranes crying in the distance. I think about my life, the roads I've traveled, the choices I've made. I've made friends and had more than my share of adventures, but there's a lonely place in my heart, and I hide behind a mask.

A voice in my head just asked me what I was running from. It was a gentle voice, not like the others.

I'm afraid, God, I'm afraid. I'm running because I'm afraid, afraid of getting what's coming to me. I'm running because I'm not strong enough to fight.

January 28, 1949

Friday night and the Midway is hopping. It's exciting, crowds of smiling people, expecting the next thrill, hoping for the next prize.

I'm taking tickets for a chance to ring a bell with a sledge hammer. It didn't look like anyone could do it, hours went by and most barely hit the bell-ringer half way. Then a short stocky man came up with a group of other men and said, "Let me show you how it's done." He rang the bell with one whack.

I saw the same guy later, standing in front of the boxing ring, flexing his muscles and calling to the crowd, taunting them to fight with him. (A sign behind him said 'FRANKIE KOLBURN ARKANSAS WILDCAT – stay in the ring 5 minutes and YOU WIN $500 - 50 cents a chance.) He said something about a man's girlfriend that wasn't very nice, the man got mad and paid the 50 cents to get in the ring. I thought to myself, "Mister, how stupid can you be?"

music fills the cotton candy air

I had to turn my head more than once: leg shows, gambling dens, smooth talking barkers. Father would not approve.

January 29, 1949

Made friends with a family of Indians—Big Chief Little Bear is one of the wrestlers. He and his family live in a trailer they pull behind a pick-up truck. He saw me sitting by myself after the carnival closed last night and came to sit beside me. He introduced himself and asked if I was traveling alone. "I have my dog Suzie," I said.

He nodded, then asked, "Are you new to carnie life?" I told him I was new enough that I still had a lot to learn. He invited me to come to his trailer for coffee in the morning. Said Mrs. Little Bear would probably have biscuits.

January 30, 1949

His wife have did indeed have biscuits, with scrambled eggs, and grits as well. Afterwards Big Chief and I went outside. He offered me a folding chair and said quietly, "I want to give you some advice. Be careful who you call friend." Then he talked for a good ten minutes, telling me about cheats and card sharks, women who would use me, then stab me in the back, and the games of 'no chance' rigged to take my money.

I thanked him for the warning, but I'm not as stupid as I look.

February 2, 1949

We had the last couple days off, a lot of drinking and card playing. I try to keep to myself.

Big Chief came by my tent and asked if I wanted some company. Not really but what could I say? The man likes to talk.

He told me the Arkansas Wildcat's story. "He was a world class boxer and wrestler. Then he got in trouble with the mafia, was fighting in the Golden Gloves in Chicago, and they told him to throw the fight—they had their money on the other guy. Well, Frankie knocked him out on the first punch. Needless to say, he got out of town in a hurry. He changed his name and started traveling with carnivals, boxing in county fairs. We show him some extra respect; he could beat the tar out of any of us.

February 4, 1949

The boss has me running the Ferris wheel. I take tickets, check that people are buckled in, turn it on and off. I enjoy the music playing while the wheel turns, the excited faces of the children and couples in love. This has to be one of the best jobs I've ever had.

Walking around during my break, I noticed a sign advertising the world's fattest lady - 25 cents. I wondered how she feels, being a freak show, then decided she probably feels about like I do. So I spent the 25 cents meet her. She stared at me for a while, then said, "You work here, don't you?" She explained that though she doesn't go outside, she watches from the window. "Come back tomorrow after 5:00 if you want. We can talk."

February 5, 1949

It was that time of day when shadows are long that I knocked on the fat lady's door. A man's voice called to come in. When I went in, I looked around for a man, but it turns out the fat lady isn't a lady after all.

He laughed and said, "Don't look so surprised! It's all fake, everything. It's whatever will make the most money. The boss says people would rather gawk and point at a woman who weighs 700 pounds than a man. So here I am, a phony carnival freak.

"And you, you came to stare and think you're better."

I told him I didn't, I knew how it felt to be phony and a freak. He didn't say anything, then got red in the face and started yelling, "You don't know shit! Get out you damn liar—get out!"

Then he started laughing, and I heard him call in a woman's voice as I closed the door, "See you in the funny papers!"

February 6, 1949

We tore down and packed up today, started at 8:00 this morning and finished about midnight. Don't think I want to make a living as a carnie.

AUBURN, ALABAMA

February 8, 1949

We've moved on to Auburn, Alabama. Looks like a quiet town. Rode through some beautiful country to get here.

February 9, 1949

Spent the day setting up, my back is killing me.

A fight outside the food tent. Well, not much of a fight. Frankie knocked a guy out then shouted to the rest of us, "Don't wave your fists at me, unless you plan to use them!"

February 10, 1949

A new sideshow has joined us – Maury's Trapeze Artists. A man swings 60 feet in the air upside down, holding a rope by his teeth as his wife swings on the other end, also holding on with her teeth. Of course, there's a safety net, and at the end of each show, one of them lets go on purpose so she'll fall into the net—then she jumps up and bows. The crowd loves it.

February 11, 1949

Working in the food tent, filling trays of gumbo and grits, I saw the Maury's. He looked like he'd had too much to drink—she took his tray from him when it looked like he was about to spill it. Then he started cussing her, called her a whore. She threw his tray in his face, gumbo and grits going everywhere. He then flipped her tray up against her, spilling food all over her costume. About that time, Frankie came up behind him and picked him up by his belt and the back of his neck, carried him to the door, and threw him out in one swoop. Everybody started cheering except his wife, who ran out crying.

Later that night, I saw Mr. Maury staggering down Midway, waving his bottle of Del Rio Port, saying, "Lookie here at the señorita on the label. She's the woman for me!"

February 12, 1949

Big Chief's daughter Irene sat next to me in the food tent and asked if she could borrow $20.00. She said she'd be in real danger if she didn't come up with some money fast. "I'll pay you back, one way or another." She winked and touched my leg. I told her I didn't have that kind of money. "Have you asked your dad?"

"No, I don't want him to know. Please don't say anything! You have to have something. I know you got paid today. I'll make it worth your while," she whispered as she snuggled up to my arm.

About that time, Frankie came over and called her a slut, and she jumped up to slap him. He grabbed her arm and pushed her back in the chair. Then she started cussing a blue streak, and I decided to disappear out the back.

February 14, 1949

Frankie came to my tent and said, "Whatever you do, don't give that bitch Irene any money. She's hooked on drugs, her arms are pincushions, and she's probably slept with every man here, who knows what she's got. You give her money, she'll play you like a fiddle."

I don't know what to do. I don't want to give her money, but I don't want a scene either. Maybe it's time for me to skip town.

February 16, 1949

Dammit I can't find my money – someone must have taken it when I was working the Midway.

I reported it to the boss. All he said was, "Do I look like a cop? You want to report it, go to the police station."

The police station is the last place I want to go, so looks like they'll keep my money, and I worked my butt off for nothing.

February 17, 1949

Tommy came to the Tilt-a-Whirl while I was taking tickets and whispered, "I think I should tell you something." He looked around and said, "I saw Big Chief Little Bear coming out of your tent the other night."

So now I'm mad as hell, but what can I do? Big Chief's bigger than I am and knows how to fight. Might as well get used to being broke again.

February 18, 1949

Tommy came to my tent crying, his eyes black and blue, his lips swollen. I asked what happened. He said, "Irene was standing behind us at the Tilt-a-Whirl when I told you about Big Chief. She told him I snitched—he said he was teaching me a lesson." He sobbed, "I want to go home!"

"Natchez is only 400 miles from here," he went on. "We can hitchhike there in a day if the rides are right. Will you come with me? Please, I don't want to go alone."

NATCHEZ, MISSISSIPPI

February 22, 1949

To get to Tommy's wasn't easy traveling after all. Our first ride was a sonofabitch who wanted me to pay him. When I told him I was broke, he started cussing and called me a low-down bastard. Stopped and told us to get out in the middle of nowhere.

Then a storm came up, and we got soaked before we finally found an old produce stand to get in. I bet it rained for 24 hours straight, nothing to eat or to start a fire with. Temperature dropped, and we were freezing cold. Tommy started crying, and I couldn't do anything but curl up in a ball, told Tommy to do the same, Suzie between us, and we survived the night.

The sun came out this morning, we started walking west along highway 20, and it wasn't long before a pickup truck stopped and let us hop in the back. He brought us the rest of the way here.

February 23, 1949

Tommy's mom was so glad to see him, she said, "I need to whip you good!" then hugged him and wouldn't let go. She thanked me for bringing him home.

"I don't know how I can repay you," she said. I told her she didn't need to. "The least I can do is feed you. And both of you could use a bath and your clothes washed. You can call me Ann."

February 24, 1949

Ann fixed me a bed on the back porch, says if I'll help out around the place, my dog and I can stay as long as we need to.

February 25, 1949

Went to the jungle, to see who was there, left a message for Bonnie.

February 28, 1949

I'm in bed with a cough and tired to the bone. I feel like a cement block is on my chest, and I just want to sleep.

My lungs haven't been right since the double pneumonia in Texas and then almost drowning in Florida. God, how much longer do I have?

March 1, 1949

Suzie's sick. I've put her in bed with me but she just shivers, looks at me with the saddest eyes.

March 3, 1949

Suzie's worse, hasn't eaten for days, barely lifts her head when I talk to her.

March 7, 1949

Ann took one look at Suzie and said she was wormy. "I can take care of that," she said, "Garlic tea with ginger root."

March 15, 1949

Suzie's better, but I feel half-dead.

March 24, 1949

Haven't changed clothes, shaved, or combed my hair in 2 weeks. If I don't get out of bed, Ann says she's calling the authorities. I don't think I have the strength. Just let them kill me.

March 25, 1949

Bonnie came looking for me, got the message in the jungle I was in town. She expressed herself in no uncertain terms, I needed to snap out of it and come with her to Nashville. Maybe that was all the tonic I needed.

I cleaned myself up, she gave me a haircut—she's got some business in the jungle, then Nashville, here we come.

I said good-bye to Tommy and wished him well. I apologized to Ann for having to put up with me. She said, "No hard feelings, I hope you get better."

Bonnie and I walked out to highway and stuck out our thumbs. Didn't take long to get a ride.

Now we're in the back of a pick-up. Nothing so soothing as watching the miles go by.

A cloud peeks over the trees. If it had a voice, it'd be soft and saying, you're not alone.

Tennessee River – reminds me of Laura's arms, wide and held out for her children.

NASHVILLE, TENNESSEE

March 27, 1949

I look up from my writing to see the moon is watching me.

Bonnie and I are camping beside Otter Creek south of Nashville. We've made two separate lean-tos with branches and canvas, a campfire between us.

Hauling Bonnie's trunk along is a pain in the butt, but the woman does know how to pack for travel. Nothing like toasting with a glass of wine and a shot of her 'rhumatiz' medicine before settling down for the night.

March 28, 1949

She pointed me in the direction of a tobacco farm to look for work. Said she had some business in Nashville and would be back at suppertime.

Spent three hours hoeing tobacco for a farmer with the name Alexander on the mailbox, made enough to buy us some groceries.

March 29, 1949

Back at Alexander's tobacco farm – he says I can work the rest of the week. Bonnie and I are comfortable enough camping. She spends the day doing who knows what. I buy the food (or catch it from the creek) and she cooks it.

Hank Williams on the radio. I'm so lonesome I could die, too, but then Suzie rubs her head against my leg. At least my dog loves me.

April 2, 1949

Bonnie came back to camp and announced she was packing up and leaving Nashville tonight, her business is finished here—going to try to jump a northbound. "Join me if you want," she said, "The train leaves in an hour."

PADUCAH, KENTUCKY

April 4, 1949

I gather my thoughts
to watch them wander
like butterflies in
a field of flowers

Ms. Bonnie has a lady's hands
They dance as she speaks

She gave me one of her snuff cans. She also gave me a half smile and a look that said 'don't ask.'

Watching the campfire, my mind sparkles like the flames, ignited with ideas and good thoughts.

April 5, 1949

Hard to believe Bonnie's almost 70 – and can still jump a slow-moving train. I don't forget to call her ma'am.

KARNAK, ILLINOIS

April 6, 1949

We're laying low in the jungle. A tramp attacked a local farmer; then the farmer chased the tramp with a pitchfork and killed him.

April 10, 1949

Hobo in the jungle tonight telling stories about the names of towns he's visited (Burnt Prairie, Mays Lick, America). I'm sitting back with my journal and book of Louis L'Amour poems, alternating between listening to him and reading. I don't feel much like being sociable.

Suzie, on the other hand, has made friends with everyone in the jungle.

LINCOLN, ILLINOIS

April 12, 1949

Fond farewell this morning - Bonnie said, you know where to find me. She handed me another snuff can.

Cherry's moved to southern Illinois – too bad I'm going the other direction.

Another hobo said he was going to the convention in Britt – I asked if he'd take a message to Laura when he goes through Belle Plaine. Ask her to meet me behind the A & P August 1st at noon. Tell her I want to talk to her.

I wonder if she'll take me back.

DIXON, ILLINOIS

April 14, 1949

Hitchhiked to Dixon, went to the Morrison Hotel to see about working for food, but the hotel's closed for some reason. I know where else I can get a meal. Heading out to.

April 15, 1949

Made camp beside the spring.

April 16, 1949

Walked to the Morrisons. Mrs. Morrison had beef and noodles and gooseberry pie. She invited me to stay for supper, which of course I did.

Shorty said if I was looking for work, he and the neighbors could use help planting corn and soybeans.

April 17, 1949

Went to say hello to the Lehman's, let them know I was back in the area. Oscar asked where I was staying. When I told him, he said he had a good Army tent I could use.

April 24, 1949

Another hobo in the neighborhood, walks around wearing bib overalls and a neck tie with no shirt. Helen says he's loony as a bird, in and out of the state hospital, but he's Isaac's Livingstone's's father, so people are good to him.

I met him at the Morrison's. They treat him like they do me, free meals and a couch to sleep on. He doesn't work though, just tells one tall tale after another. The girls seem to enjoy hearing him talk. I didn't say anything, but there's no way his cousin is Jesse James and they have a hide-out up the creek.

Some news that was a surprise to me. George Lehman jumped a train when he turned 18, and the family hasn't seen him since.

April 30, 1949

I've been making the rounds in the neighborhood, going from farm to farm. Everyone glad for an extra hand. Plowing, planting, spreading manure. It's work, but it's good work, and I'd like to stay until the convention in Britt.

I'm thinking about what to say to Laura, "I'm sorry, let's try again. I miss you."

Shit, she probably won't even meet me.

May 2, 1949

Mrs. Morrison's brother David has come to stay with them so another worker in the neighborhood, which is all right with me. Plenty of work, and I enjoy his company. Reminds me of myself when I was his age.

May 4, 1949

Helping in Lehman's butcher house, scraping casings for sausage.

May 9, 1949

Back at Lehman's. People bring their butchering from miles so it's a long day. I think Helen likes someone to talk to when she's scraping all those casings— she told stories about the history of this beautiful valley "There's a rich history here. Trouble is, nobody cares."

olden days whisper from
the ruins of Wilson's mill
history walks on moccasined feet

May 13, 1949

Friday the 13th and nothing bad happened.

Back at the Morrison's, fixing fences. The two oldest girls, Janie and Sharon, came and watched awhile. Janie asked me where I've traveled. When I listed some of the places, she said she'd love to travel like that. Sharon asked, "Don't you have a family?" With a lump in my throat, I said, "Just my dog Suzie.

May 23, 1949

Went to the Morrison's and offered to hoe the garden. The girls came out and started talking at once, telling how their dad was in a car accident. He was all right, but the woman in the other car was killed, and Shorty wasn't talking to anyone. Janie said she'd never seen her daddy cry before.

I felt his grief settle over the day, a dark cloud covering the sunshine.

June 12, 1949

walking the path
alone with my thoughts
a shadow follows

June 23, 1949

Big birthday party for the Morrison twins, who turned 10 today. Picnic in the yard, fried chicken, potato salad, chocolate cake. All the Lehmans were there.

When I left, Suzie didn't come with me, but took off after the girls. I called a couple times, but she wouldn't come. Damn dog, I didn't realize how lonely this campsite would be without her.

June 28, 1949

Suzie is staying with the Morrisons, running behind the girls on their bikes, letting them dress her in girl clothes. She was glad to see me, but when the girls took off, she went with them.

July 24, 1949

Not paying attention, I stepped on a copperhead—he missed, but my heart stopped anyway. Reminds me of the last verse in Emily Dickinson's "Snake."

> *But never met this fellow,*
> *Attended or alone,*
> *Without a tighter breathing,*
> *And zero to the bone.*

Bobwhite quail, bob*white*, bob-bob*white*

covey of quail
startled by my step;
flee skyward
  in every direction

I've made a bouquet for Laura—Queen Anne's lace and purple clover. Wondering if I can go back, wondering if she'll have me.

Looks like I'm leaving without Suzie. She enjoys the Morrison girls more than me, and I don't have the heart to make her come.

BELLE PLAINE, IOWA

August 3, 1949

Found Bo, the town drunk, and asked him if he knew anything about Laura Martinson. He said, "Yeah, she's living above the phone company, working the switchboard. I think she's got a boyfriend too. Leroy Krantz's Model T is parked in front for days at a time.

A punch in my stomach took my breath away. When I didn't speak, he said, "Sorry Buddy, that wasn't what you wanted to hear."

August 4, 1949

I didn't have the nerve to meet Laura after all. I watched from an alley down the street. She waited about a half hour, then laid an envelope down and left.

Inside were some photographs that she'd had copied the size of postage stamps. Said she thought I'd like to have them, pictures from my childhood, my parents, grandparents, aunts, and uncles, our wedding picture. There was one of Dorene about seven years old, pulling a little boy who looked like me in a wagon, with the name Gerald Dean at the bottom. And the last was her confirmation picture.

I can't stop crying.

August 4, 1949

I'm memorizing Frost's poem, "The Road Not Taken," to recite at Britt.

BRITT, IOWA

August 5, 1949

Another great reunion. Glad to see Kathy, Fritz, Fog, and Jim here from Texas. Look forward to three nights of jungle music, poetry, storytelling, and a steady supply of mulligan.

Picked up the latest Hobo Directory and saw that Boskey Jan left an address for Boskeydell. Wondering and hoping that means she's gone back home.

I was nominated for Hobo King (I do a pretty good job reciting poetry) but was running against Jim who's better looking, and he won. So Jim is the new official King of the Road. He laughed and said I could be his attendant.

August 6, 1949

Connecticut Red announced a poetry festival in the jungle in Abilene, Kansas next weekend. Fog and Jim say we should all go, call ourselves the Long Lost Poets Society. We all liked the name and the idea, so we're planning to ride a gondola car, weather permitting. Me, Fog, Kathy, Jim, and Fritz, sitting on top of the world.

ABILENE, KANSAS

August 7, 1949

"The trail is the thing, not the end of the trail. Travel too fast, and you miss all you are traveling for." Louis L'Amour

We started out on the train's gondola car, admiring the wide-open sky, but ended up riding the brake rod underneath to keep from getting caught—bulls everywhere.

Then there was a fight on the train, a young smart aleck was pushed off and probably killed. Not the scenic and peaceful trip we'd hoped for.

Jumped off train just before it stopped in Abilene. Set about to find the jungle.

August 8, 1949

Spending the night in the jungle. I've gone off by myself. Lonely without Suzie, but does feeling sorry for myself change anything?

on a cloudy evening
a swooping hawk
a rabbit's cry

August 10, 1949

"The swiftest traveler is he that goes afoot," Henry David Thoreau

A group of migrant workers heading to California joined us in the jungle. One played the spoons that sounded just like a train click-clacking along the tracks. He sang this song a few times, until we could sing it with him.

just moving nothing else
just moving
rhythm of train
rocking my world
not a worry when I'm moving
moving on

One of the men introduced himself as Dust Bowl Troubadour. He played a guitar and taught us a song he called "Hobo Lullaby" – so beautiful, I'm copying the first verse.

> Go to sleep you weary hobo
> Let the towns drift slowly by
> Can't you hear the steel rails hummin'
> That's the hobo's lullaby

August 15, 1949

Dammit. I missed the train. The others got on ahead of me, but my foot slipped as I was trying to jump on. Lucky I didn't get killed or have my legs cut off. Fog waved from the side of the box car, "Catch the next one, Buddy!"

Went back to the jungle in a piss-poor mood.

August 16, 1949

Dust Bowl came over to where I was eating the morning mulligan (warmed over from last night). He said, "Hang in there, Swede, just follow your footsteps, and don't let things get to you—we're all in this together." He handed me a piece of paper, "Here's a poem I'm working on, trying to make a song out of it. Tell me what you think." Then he started singing, "This land is your land, this land is my land..."

After he left, I cleaned myself up, packed my bedroll and satchel, and headed out.

TEXARKANA, TEXAS

August 20, 1949

Riding on top of a freight car, my face to the wind.

Texas shines a bright greeting
afternoon sun on red river

red earth
runs to the river
and calls it by name

Things might work for me after all.

AUSTIN, TEXAS

August 22, 1949

Found the jungle, but something didn't feel right. Then I saw the sign for 'get out fast' so that's exactly what I did.

Went to a diner to see if I could wash dishes for food. A guy sitting at the counter said, "Come here, Buddy, and order up what you want. I'll pay for it." Music to a hobo's ears.

He told me it was a pleasure to make my acquaintance, called me an American icon, whatever that means. Then he invited me to come behind the building, said he had something he wanted to see. I followed him, but once we were outside, he turned around with a different face, all twisted and angry. He held a knife under my throat and called me a sorry good-for-nothing shit and said the world would be a better place without me. He tied my hands behind me, knotted a scarf around my mouth, and shoved me behind some trash barrels. He said he'd be back after dark. "We'll go for a walk!" and he laughed with the same hateful laugh I hear in my head, when voices yell at me to die.

I knew he was going to kill me, and God wouldn't stop him. I prayed anyway because I couldn't think of anything else to do, and God must have listened, because in about 20 minutes, a cook from the diner found me when he came to throw out the trash. He untied me and told me to scram.

I don't think I've ever moved faster.

August 23, 1949

Found a mission with cots to sleep on, soup, and bread. A man introduced himself as Pastor Jack and gave me a commodity bag with a Bible, toothbrush, soap, and a razor. He offered me clothes; mine were looking a little rough. When he asked for a donation, I turned my pockets inside out.

August 29, 1949

Dammit, I must've got lice at the mission, either from the bed or the clothes they gave me. Every inch of my body is crawling and itching, driving me crazier than I already am.

Went back to the mission for a scalding bath in bleach water. Pastor Jack was nowhere to be seen.

September 1, 1949

Not finding any work, the only handout is at the mission, and I'm trying to avoid that place. I've been going through garbage, sleeping in dark corners. I need to get out of here.

September 4, 1949

A heavy cloud covers me; I can barely breathe. I haven't slept or eaten in three days. I'm going to kill myself; I can't live like this. I'm sick and tired of this miserable life. I think standing in front of a train would be the quickest way. I probably wouldn't feel a thing.

September 5, 1949

I laid across the tracks last night and closed my eyes, wanting to die with all my heart. I cried and prayed for about a half hour before I heard a train whistle, long and lonesome in the distance. I listened as it got closer, felt the tracks vibrate, and waited for it to hit me and end it all. Then I swear, Dorene, I heard your voice scream, "Daddy!" I couldn't go through with it and rolled off the tracks just in time.

All I can do is put one foot in front of the other.

•

RICHMOND, TEXAS

September 14, 1949

A railroad bull saw me jump from the train in Crabb and told me he was informing me that riding a train without a ticket is illegal in Texas." The last thing I remember is a 2 x 4 swinging toward my head.

I woke up on a screened-in porch with a woman standing over me. "There you are—we didn't know if you were going to make it. That bull got you pretty bad.

I didn't feel much like talking, but she kept on, "I'm a cook here at the George Ranch. The Georges let my husband and me take left-overs to the jungle in Crabb. It was my husband who carried you here. You got friends in the jungle, you know. Cotton-eyed Kathy, Texas Jim, Fog Man, Flagstaff Fritz, we know them well, and they all spoke for you, said you were a gentleman. Fritz made sure you got your satchel."

All I knew was my head was pounding.

"They said your hobo name is Dakota Swede. I'm known as Lunchbox Lana in the jungle because I like to share my good cooking when I can. You're lucky to be here."

Her husband came in then, a wide-shouldered man who probably had no trouble carrying me. He introduced himself as Don Kall, said if I have any trouble just call – his laugh matched his size.

September 16, 1949

I'm sitting on the porch listening to Mrs. George play the piano, "The Yellow Rose of Texas," "Red River Valley," "Buffalo Gals." I'm going to get better here.

September 19, 1949 My Birthday

Lana takes good care of me. Three meals a day on a tray and friendly company to boot.

September 23, 1949

Up and moving. My head still hurts but I can take care of myself again. I *am* a lucky man. I'd heard about the George Ranch before and thought I'd like to work here. Well, not only can I work here for as long as I want, I get food and lodging too.

September 27, 1949

They've moved me to the Batch House, short for Bachelor's Quarters, where the cowboys live. I'm no cowboy so I think they just want me off the porch. Don said don't worry, I'll still get Lana's cooking.

September 28, 1949

I'm living with two cowboys. I was surprised how young they were. They laughed and the older one said that's why we're called "cow-*boys.*"

"My name is Caleb. I'm 14, and this is Wyatt. He's 12." Wyatt tipped his hat and said, "Pleased to meet you, sir." I noticed they both had a plug of tobacco under their bottom lip.

They're busy with fall round up, roping calves to get them ready for a drive to Abilene. "Castrating, branding, vaccinating, and dehorning, it's a lot of work," Caleb said, "We'll take all the help we can get."

I told him I was better at cleaning stalls. He shrugged and told me to help myself.

October 1, 1949

Pastor Ron from a church in Thompson came to visit. He put his hand on my shoulder and prayed for God to touch me. All I could say was amen.

October 3, 1949

Enjoying the quiet, boys out doing something, and I'm just here, rocking on the porch.

October 8, 1949

I went to the main house this morning to see if Miss Mamie had any work for me. She said she could probably find something, but first she wanted me to sample the cookies Lana had cooling— "Joe Froggers," she called them, "They're a favorite around here, the recipe is handed down from my great-grandmother, who probably got it from her great-grandmother, ginger cookies the size of lily pads, made with molasses and rum."

One bite, and I knew why they were a favorite.

Joe Frogger Cookies

1/3 cup dark rum
1 tablespoon water

1 ½ teaspoon salt
3 cups flour
¾ teaspoon ground ginger
½ teaspoon ground allspice
¼ teaspoon ground nutmeg
1/8 teaspoon ground cloves
1 cup dark molasses
1 teaspoon baking soda
½ cup butter
1 cup sugar

Mix well and refrigerate at least 8 hours. Preheat oven to 375 degrees. Line two baking sheets with parchment paper. Roll out and cut into 4-inch circles. Space about 1 ½ inches apart on baking sheets. Bake 6 -7 minutes. Cool on baking sheets for 10 minutes, then transfer to wire racks.

October 22, 1949

Don and Lana stopped to see if we needed anything from town. Caleb gave her a list, then she asked if I wanted to come along. "Might be good to get out for a while." I thought so too, so I rode in the back seat of their new Ford on the way to Richmond.

Lana was driving so Don could turn around and visit. He told me I couldn't have picked a better place to stay. He said that the George's were known for caring for the less fortunate. "As a matter of fact, Mrs. George keeps the door to the smoke house unlocked and open. She says if anyone's hungry enough to steal food, they can have it."

He went on, "Mr. George wants us to shop for new spurs and hats for the cowboys. He said, 'Just put it on my bill.' Not many ranch owners will do that.

"And he wants us to buy a vacuum cleaner for Miss Mamie—he's tired of her fussing about cigarette ashes on the carpet and doesn't want to be bothered with an ashtray."

December 25, 1949 Christmas Day

Mrs. Mamie had the cooks set up a meal outside the Batch House and invited all the hired help, including the sharecroppers and their families for a meal to remember – roast goose, green beans, sweet potato pone, sourdough biscuits, and plum pudding. The best part was everyone got a gift, the cowboys got spurs and hats, the sharecroppers got leather Bible covers, the cooks got knitted scarves, and I got a book of poems by Conrad Aiken *The Divine Pilgrim*.

January 12, 1950

Most beautiful day at Brazos Lake, alone with my journal. I watch sun-sparkled ripples float across the water, a family of ducks swim by, and I think what peace, more than I ever imagined. Writing a letter to Jan, letting her know where I am.

January 16, 1950 Happy Birthday, Dorene

You're 17 today.

yellow butterfly forgets
it's winter in Illinois

January 22, 1950

Today when Pastor Ron came to visit, I told him everything. How I was turned over to authorities for not providing for my family, put in jail, and left there. How I didn't eat or sleep for weeks and started hearing voices that wanted to kill me. How I ended up in a hospital for the insane and stayed there three years. How I couldn't take it anymore, jumped a train to Waterloo, and have been running ever since.

I cried and told him about my family, Laura, Dorene, and Gerald. How I missed them, how I hated myself for failing them, how most of the time I want to die, and I cried some more.

He didn't say anything for a while, then put his hand on my shoulder and said, "Swede, there's a big God who loves you." I told him I couldn't imagine why. "It doesn't matter why; what matters is that you trust Him. He says He loves you. Do you believe Him?"

I couldn't answer, but I knew he was right, like someone turned a light on. Maybe there's hope for me yet.

I shook his hand when he left and said, "You can call me Reuben."

February 11, 1950

The boys are excited about the rodeo coming up. They've been practicing roping for days—lassoing and tying calves in record time. They tried to teach me how to do it—they were holding their sides laughing by the time I gave up trying.

February 18, 1950

I can't believe I got to meet Gene Autry. Turns out he's a good friend of the George's and comes every year for the rodeo in Houston.

He was standing on the front porch, wearing a blue knit suit and a shirt embroidered with half-moons and stars. I recognized him right away.

He must have noticed the surprised look on my face. He laughed, held out his hand, and said, "Hello, I'm Gene Autry, and it's nice to meet you!" His voice sings, just like on the radio.

February 25, 1950

Miss Mamie had the chuckwagon crew roast a whole hog. The cowboys put hay bales around a bonfire, and Mr. Autry sang cowboy songs. "Happy Trails to You" I felt like he sang just for me.

March 1, 1950

Lana told me that the Georges have a house guest, a famous mystery writer from Cornwall. He wants to use a Texas ranch as the setting for his next book. She heard him telling the Georges about it, with cattle rustlers, horse thieves, and gun fights. Mr. George laughed and told him he had quite an imagination. He said, "The only cattle rustling ever done at the George Ranch was by a couple of cowhands who had too much to drink. They made so much noise, Miss Mamie called the sheriff, had them arrested, and that was the end of that."

March 3, 1950

Planted Miss Mamie's spring garden, fed and watered the cattle, a Brahman-Shorthorn mix that Mr. George breeds himself.

March 4, 1950

This was some day. The children were admiring a newborn calf when I heard a bellow and saw the Brahma mother charging toward them, head down. I didn't think, just took off with the shovel that was in my hand and got to them just in time to smack the cow upside the head hard enough that it stumbled, and the children were able to run and duck under the fence. I was close behind.

After supper, Mr. George invited me to his Trophy Room with stuffed animals on every wall. He offered me a cigar and a bourbon.

I said no thanks to the bourbon, but yes to the cigar. He shook my hand and thanked me for the rescue.

March 6, 1950

Mr. George wants me to sign up for Social Security, says he'll give me a full-time job that I can retire from. Now that's something to think about. They can't still be looking for me after all these years.

March 9, 1950

Now I can say I've been to Houston. Went with Mr. George to sign up for Social Security, first time I've signed my name in years. Decided while I was at it, to get a post office box too.

My running days are over.

April 3, 1950

Miss Mamie invited me to live one of the sharecropper houses. I can work and do odd jobs in exchange for rent.

I'm living good, Dorene.

April 9, 1950 Easter Sunday

Ranch picnic with ham, deviled eggs, green beans, corn pudding, on the side lawn under the big tree house. Colored eggs dot the landscape.

Musicians played spoons, jugs, and harmonicas. Daniel, lead singer for the ranch, played a small guitar and sang song after song, "Turkey in the Straw," "Goober Peas," "She'll be Coming 'Round the Mountain." The cowboys started dancing, and I joined right in.

April 10, 1950

Made a new friend—one of the sharecroppers stopped by to introduce himself, said, "Just call me Uncle Bob. Everyone else does!" Maybe in his late 60's, white beard covers his chest. He brought a tin of dominoes and asked if I played.

He said to be on the lookout for a big rat snake, raiding his chickens and eating all their eggs. "That's food off my table and money out of my pocket. I'm offering a reward for its capture."

April 16, 1950

Went to Uncle Bob's this afternoon—he caught the rat snake, is keeping him in a bobcat cage on the front porch, and has named him Sammy.

April 29, 1950

Miss Mamie's niece was killed in car accident, a heavy cloud over everything today. My heart is broken with the family's.

Sitting in the treehouse, I remember the day Mary and the other children invited me to see it, remembering the laughter and the rhymes for me—I remember the clapping games, Miss Mary Mack, and now… there's nothing but a black hole in my heart

Even the clouds weep.

May 10, 1950

Got a call from a young woman in Illinois yesterday evening. Said she was looking for her grandfather who disappeared in 1939. I said, "Honey, I'm not your grandfather," and hung up.

I sat for the longest time, just looking at the phone. It hurts too much to write.

May 18, 1950

Have a headache this morning—I think I'm getting worse instead of better.

Visited the Lutheran Church in Richmond Sunday. Looking through the hymnal, I came across "When I Have Sung my Song," written by my uncle Johann Elner. I haven't sung it since I was a child; it's a song about dying. I'm singing now—

When sunset ends and day is done
And twilight fades away,
It's then I'll sing my evening song
And send my thoughts afar—

May 22, 1950

Got a letter from Jan Curry. Good news, she's back home, in school to be a teacher. Said it didn't take her long to realize marriage to Drifter was a big mistake. She wrote to her dad who wired her the money to come home.

June 9, 1950

Jim and Fog came to visit today, wanted to share their newest poems and talk about life in general. I told them I haven't been writing much, but I did share one of Frost's poems I like.

Away

and I may return
if dissatisfied
with what I learn
from having died

June 23, 1950

The pain in my head doesn't go away.

I'm not afraid to die—just hope I remember that when the time comes.

June 26, 1950

Spent the morning behind a mule, guiding a hand plow with the name John Deere painted on the handle. That means it's a good plow, but my head is pounding and my back is killing me. I'm going to bed.

September 16, 1950 My Birthday

I don't get off the porch. People bring me things to do – cleaning cotton, cracking pecans.
My head hurts more when I'm on my feet.

September 18, 1950

Another blinding headache. I see a bright hot light when I close my eyes.

September 20, 1950

That woman from Illinois called again, said she wanted to check again since Rueben Martinson wasn't a common name, especially with the same birthday. She asked if I ever lived in Luzerne, Iowa, and was it possible I lost my memory? She went on about her mother Dorene, how her father disappeared when she was six, escaped from an insane asylum in Independence, Iowa and never seen again, how she always wondered why he didn't come back. I held the receiver to my ear and tried to think what to say.

I put the phone down and walked away.

Appendix

September 30, 1950

Dear Dorene,

My good friend Reuben Martinson asked me to send this satchel to an address in Belle Plaine, Iowa, with your name and a message to "Please Forward." I hope it finds its way to you.

I'm sorry to say that Reuben passed away last Tuesday. He took to bed with a headache and wouldn't let me call a doctor. I was with him at the end. He wanted me to tell you, he always loved you.

Best wishes,

Lana Kall
(Lunchbox Lana)

Social Security Records

Name: Reuben Martinson
Birth date: September 16, 1899

Social Security Number: 387-05-7261
Occupation: Farm Laborer
Death Date: September 24, 1950
Death Location: George Ranch, Richmond, Texas

Lars and Anna Matilda Martinson

Reuben Martinson birth place, Hample, North Dakota
Lars Martinson in center, with Reuben and Hildur

Lars with Reuben and Hildur

Reuben and Hildur

Hildur Martinson in center

Reuben and Laura Martinson

Dorene Martinson

Gerald and Dorene Martinson

Dorene Martinson, confirmation

Bibliography

Blakley, Joanne, "Carl and I," "Walking 6th Street," "Greetings, Lone Bird," "Prayer for Peace," "Lesson of the Butterfly," "Texas Bayou," "To Kit Carson, Wherever You Are," *On the Road Home, Travel Poems,* Chaplain Publishing, 2008

Blakley, J., "Reuben, Reuben," *The Writer's Voice, Anthology of Poetry and Prose,* Southern Illinois Writers Guild, Chaplain, Publishing, 2009

Blakley, J. "The Legend of Davy Getz," "Gladstone," "Ancient Dwelling," *Distilled Lives, Illinois State Poetry Society 20th Anniversary Anthology,* Illinois State Poetry Society, 2011

Cummings, E. E., "i carry your heart," *Complete Poems,* Liveright Publishing, 1932

Dickinson, Emily, "To Make a Prairie," "Snake," *The Poems of Emily Dickinson,* Harvard University Press, 1951

Dooley, Carol, "Winter Flowers," unpublished

Elner, Johann, "When I Have Sung my Song," copyright J.E. Elner, used with permission

Erbsen, Wayne, *Singing Rails, Railroadin' Songs, Jokes, and Stories,* Native Ground Music, Inc., 1997

Farmer's Almanac, Almanac Publishing, 1940, 1943

Fox, "Reefer" Charles Elmer, *Tales of an American Hobo,* University of Iowa Press, 1989

Robert Frost, "Stopping by the Woods," "In the Clearing," "The Road Not Taken," *New Hampshire,* Henry Holt & Co., 1923

Graham, "Steam Train" Maury, *Tales of the Iron Road,* Paragon House, 1990

Guthrie, Woody "Hobo Lullaby," "This Land is Your Land," Woody Guthrie Publications, Inc. 1956

"Hobo Code of Ethics," www.hobo.com

Lambert, Jim, "Waiting for Life to Unfold," unpublished

L'Amour, Angelique, *A Trail of Memories, the Quotations of Louis L'Amour,* Bantam Books, 1988

L'Amour, Louis, "An Ember in the Dark," *Smoke from this Alter,* Lusk Publishing, 1939

Penn Warren, Robert, "Heart of Autumn," Louisiana State University Press, 1998

Sandburg, Carl, "Wherever Bees," *The Complete Poems of Carl Sandburg,* Harcourt, Brace & Co., 1970

Steele, Lorren, "Harvest Train," Union County Writers Group Anthology, 2008

About the Author

Joanne Blakley has taught creative and academic writing to international students at Southern Illinois and Auburn Universities. A hobo at heart, her favorite things are road trips (especially with grandchildren), hiking, journaling, and writing poetry.

She's published *On the Road Home, Travel Poems,* and *Catfish are in the Elkhorn, Helen Lehman Reminisces.* Her poems have appeared in anthologies of the Illinois State Poetry Society, Southern Illinois Writer's Guild, and Shawnee Hills Writers Group.

Lightning Source UK Ltd.
Milton Keynes UK
UKHW041821040621
384904UK00007BA/865/J

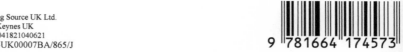

9 781664 174573